THE TRAFFIC LIGHT

~

And Five Other Stories

JACK DOPP

Illustrations by Michael Dopp

Chapbook Press

Schuler Books
2660 28th Street SE
Grand Rapids, MI 49512
(616) 942-7330
www.schulerbooks.com

The Traffic Light – And Five Other Stories

ISBN 13: 9781966196136

Library of Congress Control Number: 2025906604

Illustrations by Michael Dopp

Printed in the United States.

DEDICATION

I am dedicating these six short fables to my wife of 53 years, Janis Faye Dopp. Janis, my life's partner, passed away on October 12,2023. A dependable and accurate Editor of my writing, Janis corrected when necessary and encouraged when prudent. An English major at Indiana University, Janis had a high standard of excellence. She was an intelligent master of the written word and was by nature a particular agent of perfection. Although Janis tolerated my strange sense of humor and crazy imagination, she also pushed me to be accountable to proper grammar. So, it is with a grateful heart that I thank my dear wife, Janis Faye Dopp, for her high expectations, encouragement, faith, and love.

ACKNOWLEDGEMENTS

I wish to extend my gratitude to all those who have helped me on my journey by writing these six fables. First, I want to thank my children, Michael and Michele Dopp. Their unconditional love and support have provided me with a solid foundation. Their acceptance of my foibles and imperfections has kept me motivated even when self-doubt has seeped into my thoughts.

On a pragmatic note, I want to thank all my friends and family who have taken the time to read my stories. Their insightful acceptance of my unusual imagination provided me with the confidence to carry on. Specifically, I want to thank my lifelong friends Jim and Jan Mantakounis. They have read every story I have ever written. Their critiques and suggestions have become helpful guardrails for my overripe imagination. And big shout out to Amy Wolterstorff for the final editing of the fables. Her professional editing scrapped off the fine edges of my grammar and sentence structure making the stories readable.

Finally, I want to thank my good friend (45 years and continuing), Rita Riggs for giving me the freedom to dive into my imagination. Gifting me with her unpretentious joy and intelligent insights Rita has encouraged me to dig down into my inner soul. Pointing me toward my little kid, she gave me the confidence to scrape away at my adult certitudes and to embrace my inner child's creativity. Blessings to you my mentor, my muse, my friend.

Table of Contents

The Traffic Light

A busy boulevard, eight lanes across. The light will change soon and give me a chance to cross. I have crossed here before, and there is just enough time, 30 seconds, to make it across if I do not slip and fall. I stand at the ready and the light changes and I start across the eight lanes. A large Harley motorcycle pulls up to the light with a sudden stop right in front of me. I suddenly stop and my glasses come flying off and land on the pavement breaking the frame. I stoop over and pick up the pieces, but it is hard since my belly is so large. I do anyway and the light is counting down-

30,29,28.

"You are pathetic." The motorcycle rider says. "You-Are-Pathetic." He says again, just in case I did not hear it the first time. 27, 26,25.

You don't know me. You do not know that I have an apartment just down the street and I have two goldfish, Oscar and Felix, who depend on me to feed them. And that I have a big Lazy Boy chair that sits in front of my TV, and I watch Jeopardy every night at 7 pm. And I always know all the questions. 24,23,22.

 You don't know me.

I have got a friend, Fred, who meets me every Sunday at the Bagel Shop, which is just down the street. We sit and talk, my newspaper spread out between us. We solve all the problems of the world, but Fred died last Tuesday. I did not know since I never read the obituaries in the newspaper and besides I did not know Fred's last name. The cashier at the Bagel Shop told me Fred was gone. I got a bagel anyway and spread out my newspaper out in front of me and solved the problems. 21,20,19.

 You don't know me.

I was a janitor for thirty-nine years and I walked to work every day. Never missed a day. It took me 27 minutes to make the one and half mile walk. I was never late. They planned a party for me when I retired, but someone forgot to order a cake and they called off the party. I was named employee of the day twice. 18,17,16.

  You don't know me.

I went to the high school just down the street, a big school with a thousand students. They thought I was fat and didn't talk to me and when I talked, I bit my tongue. Once I stumbled in the hallway and fell into the arms of the most beautiful girl in the school. She got up and pointed her pretty finger in my face and said that I was pathetic. I bit my tongue. 15,14,13.

 You don't know me.

I grew up just down the street in that brown house with no front porch and no swing set in the backyard. My parents told me to stay in my room and be quiet, since making any noise was considered pathetic and besides, I was too fat to run and play. 12,11,10.

  You don't know me.

When I was six, I had a friend that I played with during the day and held at night. Teddy was his name. Father thought I was too old to have a friend like that, and he took him out of my arms and threw him the trash. He said Teddy was too dirty from touch and his arms were falling off and his sky-blue eyes were only holding on by a thread. Besides, he said it was "Pathetic", for a boy to have a teddy bear. 9,8,7.

It is hard to run, but time is running out. My belly is flopping back and forth as I try to run before my time is up. My legs are burning, and my chest is hurting so bad I cannot breathe. I am only halfway across the boulevard. I am falling. 6,5,4,3,2,1.

And all the drivers honk their horns and yell, "You're pathetic!"

In the emergency room the doctors and nurses gather around and someone yells, "We're losing him! Give him CPR!" A doctor begins to pound on my chest, and I try to call out," Teddy!" But no one understands. A nurse comes in to help, and she sees me and says, "Oh, so pathetic."

White fur, strong arms, and sky-blue eyes looking up at me, sitting together in peace. Ah, Teddy, you know me.

SPAGHE
SPAGHETTI
SPAGHETTI

The Masterpiece

In his first two years of Swiss Guard duty, Gabriel had encountered many vagabonds trying to sneak into the Vatican. But on the night of February 17, 1564, the old man pounding on the door of the secret entrance #12 did not seem to be a vagabond. Sure, the old guy had a rumpled cloak and a long white unruly beard, but he also had a pronounced crooked nose. Gabriel instantly recognized the intruder as no other than the great Master Michelangelo.

"Meister Michelangelo, can I help you?" Since Gabriel was all dressed up in his jester-like Swiss Guard uniform, Michelangelo had no trouble recognizing him.

"Hey, Gabe, how are ya? Say, I have been commissioned to create a work of art, and I need to get in this secret entrance."

 Gabriel unclipped his keyring from his belt and began to try various keys on the door lock.

"You know, Meister, I've never seen anyone go into this secret entrance. Why don't you try secret entrance #3 over by the pope's residence? Or secret entrance #8 over by your Sistine Chapel?"

"No, no, Gabe, I have to go in this entrance."

 After trying all his keys to no avail, Gabriel finally tried to open the door by turning the doorknob. It opened straight away. "Damn, it was open all along."

After swishing away the cobwebs from the entrance, Gabriel noticed a single candle flickering at the end of a long, dark hallway. The candle's light exposed a large room which held two large tables with several large bowls placed on top. And behind the flickering light, there appeared to be a rather large wood-burning stove.

Even though Gabriel held the door open for Michelangelo, the 88-year-old master stumbled as he crossed the threshold and entered the dark hallway. After regaining his balance, the great master turned and looked back at Gabriel. Through the darkness, Gabriel could see that Michelangelo was looking straight into his eyes. "Gabe, my commission tonight will be my greatest masterpiece. But it will not be for me or you to ever know. Gabriel, promise me that you will keep this entrance safe from vagabonds."

"I promise, Meister Michelangelo, I promise." Michelangelo closed the door and locked it from the inside.

The next night, February 18, as Gabriel was on his vagabond patrol around the Vatican, he saw someone lying in front of the secret entrance #12. As he approached, he could see that the person was covered from head to toe with white flour. When Gabriel turned the man over, his worst fears were realized—it was the great Master Michelangelo.

The great master was gasping for breath, but he managed to say one last thing to Gabriel: "Gabe, remember, keep this doorway safe from intruders."

"I promise, Meister, I promise."

And with that promise made, the creator of *David* and the painter of the Sistine Chapel ceiling passed away.

The next day Gabriel went to the scrapyard behind the Vatican. After perusing several rejected Michelangelo statues, he found just the right one for the job at hand—a sour and vengeful looking *God* that had been rejected by the Vatican because of a chip on its beard. After gathering ten of his Swiss Guard buddies, Gabriel, keeping his promise, placed the statue against the door of the secret entrance #12. It remained there, untouched, for the next 500 years.

By the year 2064, only con artists and the hopeless roamed the earth. Mankind's pollution and neglect had made the planet uninhabitable. The rising heat had turned the green fields and forests into brown deserts. The blue lakes and rivers had turned into mud. And worst of all, no child has been born in the last twenty years. Starvation and migration wars had killed off billions of people, and the only other living creatures left on the planet were possums.

The center of this world was Hoboken, New Jersey, the headquarters of Possum Plus Corporation. It was here that a chemist known to the world as the Master had developed an elixir to keep the possums of the world healthy and edible. Sliced and diced into spoon-sized glow-in-the dark cubes, possum meat had become the only food source for humans. It was not surprising, then, that Possum Plus Corporation had built high-rise possum farms across the planet.

For Randy, a Hoboken, New Jersey, native, being assigned by the Possum Guard Brigade to a remote outpost like Rome, Italy, did have some perks. The Possum Plus Corporation provided a clean cot in a 6 X 8 windowless room, access to all the possum cubes anyone could ever want to eat, and a cadre of four robots at one's command. Each of Randy's robots had its specialty.

Peter was quick, Paul was clever, and Magdalene was smart. But Randy's favorite was Judas, who was strong as an ox.

Rome, once known as the City of Fountains, had run out of water, and ever since the pope had abandoned the Vatican for the cooler climes of northern Siberia, the citizens had gone too. Since Rome's high-rise possum farm was just a few blocks from the crumbling Vatican, escaping possums would make a beeline to the ancient city to hide in the rubble and the many secret entrances.

On the night of February 18, 2064, sirens woke Randy up from a fine nightmare of less sleep. A possum had escaped from the farm, and it was Randy's turn to bring it back dead or alive. He slipped into his Possum Guard uniform: purple shorts and T-shirt with the gold letters PGB emblazoned across the chest. After grabbing his handheld remote robot controller, Randy made his way to the staging area and fired up Judas. The robots had human-like arms and legs, but their heads were circular globes that twirled around, all the better to catch wayward possums. And, of course, all the robots on earth were covered from head to toe with solar panels and never needed recharging.

Surrounded by security cameras, the Vatican had no secrets left to reveal—at least that is what Randy thought. The flashing red light in front of secret entrance #12 indicated that the stray possum had gone in that direction. When Judas and Randy arrived at the scene of the crime, they noticed possum tracks under a large marble statue in front of entrance #12.

Randy immediately yelled into his handheld robot controller, "OK, Judas, smash that statue to dust!"

"Are you sure, Randy? That statue was created by the great sixteenth-century artist Michelangelo."

"Yes, I'm sure, smash the thing to bits!"

"I mean I could just gently lift it out of the way, no problem."

"It's just a chunk of marble! Smash it!"

"Whatever you say, Randy, but I think you're making a terrible mistake."

Randy held the robot controller up to his face and yelled, "I don't give a damn what you think, Judas. Turn that marble to dust!"

"Alright already. Take it easy, man."

In a New York minute, Michelangelo's 500-year-old piece of art was smashed into rubble. And guess what? There was no possum to be found.

Randy held the controller to his mouth. "OK, I guess the fugitive must have crawled under the doorway to secret entrance #12. Do you have any objections to tearing down the secret door?"

"No, Randy."

With a single punch, Judas sent the door flying off its hinges. After brushing off a wall of ancient cobwebs from the entrance, Randy flashed a light down the dark hallway. Without any apparent drama on his mind, a baby possum stood at the end of the hallway ready to capitulate to his tormentors. Judas and Randy's journey down the dark hallway featured cobwebs dripping from the ceiling and mouse skeletons crunching underfoot. It was only when they arrived at the end of the hallway did Judas realize that they were standing in the heart of a medieval kitchen.

"Hey, look at this, Randy, this is a sixteenth-century kitchen with a large wood-burning stove."

Randy yelled into his controller, "Who cares? Just grab the varmint and let us get the hell out of this creepy place!"

Judas picked up the baby possum and threw him in his possum pouch for safekeeping. As they turned to go, Judas spotted two large tables in the kitchen. Several bowls were scattered across the surface of one table. On the other table sat a large wooden box at least six feet long and four feet wide.

Pointing to the box, Judas noticed that there was an envelope pasted on its top. "Looky here, looky here. Something is written on it."

Randy had never bothered to learn how to read, so he asked Judas to read what was written on the envelope.

"Well, sir, the envelope is addressed to you. It says, Hi, Randy, hope you are having a nice evening. This wooden box contains a giant chocolate birthday cake. It is to be delivered to my future cousin, Antonio, to celebrate his 100th birthday. He lives at the Genesis Center in Hoboken, New Jersey. Please get it to him on his birthday, March 30, Palm Sunday—Capisce? Yours truly, Michelangelo."

Randy yelled into his controller, "Do you seriously think I'm going to deliver a cake to some old fart in Hoboken? And besides, the Master would never allow that."

"Tell you what, Randy, this whole business could get you a nice holiday back in Hoboken."

Randy screamed into his controller, "How so?"

"You can play the Master like a drum, Randy. Just point out to him that a 500-year-old cake baked by Michelangelo does not come along every day, and besides a 100th birthday party would pick up the spirits of all the humans left on this miserable planet."

Randy held his controller to his mouth. "Ya think?!"

Judas placed his right arm around Randy's shoulder and waved his left hand up toward the dark hallway of the secret entrance #12. "Just imagine, Randy, going back to Hoboken and leaving Rome behind. Can you imagine it, Randy? A holiday back home and paid for by the Master."

With his controller at his side, Randy looked at Judas's waving hand and said, "Do you think, Judas, do you think?"

"Yes, my boy, yes."

Language, by 2064, had become one-English. Linguists of this language depended on the curators of such. The robots had a simple but complex approach to the language—they used simple words but with more than one thought in a sentence. "It sure was a terrible war, but not everyone was killed," they might say after a migration war. Clear, concise, and true. From lack of use, most Homo sapiens had lost the art of literacy and talked in short phases. "No way," was popular, and "Never going to happen," and "Not in this lifetime." The general tone of sapiens was negative and cynical. The Master, on the other hand, used a high-tea English accent to prove his superiority to his fellow sapiens and the robots of the world.

On March 3, 2064, Fox TV network (the only TV network remaining on the planet) broke away from a Yogi Bear cartoon for breaking news. The world knew the news had to be pretty important to interrupt the park ranger chasing Yogi around a picnic table. Using a hologram setup, the Master, broadcasting from his retreat on top of Mount Tyree, at the South Pole, revealed the discovery of Michelangelo's chocolate cake. He called the cake and Antonio's birthday a transformative and biblical moment. The Master knew darn well his citizens needed a pick-me-up. I mean, a steady diet of possum cubes and artificial water (which looked like sewage and tasted way too much like watermelon-flavored vitamin water) was more than anyone could take. The Master ended his speech by holding up the letter Michelangelo had written to Antonio. Because most sapiens of the world were illiterate, he read it aloud so all the citizens of his empire could understand the magical mystery of the moment.

Dear Antonio,

I baked this chocolate cake for your 100th birthday. Enjoy your moment.

 Sincerely,

Your distant cousin, Michelangelo

PS. It would help if you put some white icing on the cake. After all, the cake is 500 years old, and it is probably a little dry.

PPS. It might be a good idea to have lots of plastic forks available. If I do say so, everyone will want a piece of this masterpiece.

  MASTER MICHELANGELO

Just because you live 100 years does not mean you have lived 100 years. Antonio's introverted nature had justified him to a life of friendless bachelorhood. And his middling IQ qualified him for a 47-year career as a rural mail carrier (where he never met a single customer). In retirement, he lived the life of an unbaptized hermit. So, when he went down into his backyard bomb shelter when the migration wars began, no one noticed.

Antonio's twenty years in his bomb shelter were the best years of his life. Not only was he safe from four migration wars (four billion killed) and two starvations (two more billion expired), but he was able to spend his days watching reruns of *Scooby-Doo, The Waltons,* and *The Brady Bunch.* He also had a daily inspiration, offered up by his 1970 vintage boombox and a large collection of Beach Boys tapes. Oh, yes, let us not forget that Antonio had canisters filled with a twenty-year-supply of mouthwatering SpaghettiOs swimming in artificial tomato sauce.

We all have dates on our calendar that we circle – Polar Bear Swim Day, National Pig Day, or even Christmas and New Year's. For Antonio, the date that he had circled on his calendar was September 26, 2063, the day that he was going to run out of SpaghettiOs.

On September 27,' Antonio dusted off an old backpack and packed up his boombox and Beach Boys tapes along with a can opener and several plastic forks. So it was that, for the first time in twenty years, Antonio left his bomb shelter to go on a quest to find SpaghettiOs. A quest implies a journey into an alien world. Antonio's memory of the world he left behind was of green grass and weeds, of blue skies and rivers, of colorful flowers and trees, and of vibrant critters and sapiens. When Antonio pried open the door to his bomb shelter, he was greeted by an alien planet. As he gazed out at the horizon, the cloudless tangerine-colored sky bled into a brownish-orange Martian landscape. And the hot, dusty air was not fit for Homo sapiens' consumption. Worst of all was the silence—the critter less, human less, vegetation less world was drowning from a lack of good vibrations.

Scanning the horizon, Antonio sought out the familiar house, a tree, a human being—all to no avail. The drab landscape melded together with the sky, making it difficult to discern where one ended and the other began. At the juncture between earth and sky, Antonio noticed a small plume of dust. As he watched, the plume grew to a cloud and then to a dust devil that was headed straight toward him.

So, this is how my quest begins, Antonio thought to himself as he turned and ran in the opposite direction of the dust-up. As the dust cloud drew closer and closer, the shadowy source of the disturbance became clear. By 2063, most moon buggies had only two seats, but the V1037 model was a paddy wagon variation and had four seats—all the better to pick up stray vagabonds. Antonio had never been considered coordinated, and at age 99 he sure as heck could not run very well. So it was no surprise when he fell flat on his face just as the V1037 came to a skidding halt just five feet away.

"You are violating code 73247!" yelled Melvin, the Homo sapiens who was riding shotgun on the moon buggy.

The driver, Ruth the robot, stepped out of the moon buggy and walked over to Antonio. "Are you alright?" Ruth asked.

Melvin screamed into his handheld robot controller, "Don't be nice! This old fart is obviously a vagabond!"

Ruth held out her hand to Antonio. In turn, Antonio reached Ruth. Ruth's grip was firm, but her manner was gentle as she pulled Antonio to his feet. Ruth's gentle touch was a reminder to Antonio of what he had missed out on, not only over the last twenty years, but also over an entire lifetime of solitariness.

In the great canon of literature, a quest, whether it be for a holy grail, a big whale, or the best bagel in New York City, is usually not consummated until the 200th page of the book. Antonio's SpaghettiOs quest lasted two paragraphs.

"A quest for SpaghettiOs? The last SpaghettiOs were eaten years ago!" Melvin yelled.

"Sorry, Antonio, that is a fact," whispered Ruth.

"What the hell!" Antonio replied. So, not only was Antonio guilty of violating code 73247, but he was also guilty of being old. Fortuitously, Melvin and Ruth took Antonio to the only old people's home left on the planet, The Genesis Center, located right there in Hoboken. As luck would have it, the Genesis Center had a secret stash of SpaghettiOs, but alas, they had run out of the delicious morsels just hours before Antonio's arrival.

Considering that the survival rate of robots during the migration wars was in the single digits, Judas and Magdalene's wounds were tolerable. Sure, Judas had lost an arm and a leg, and Magdalene had had her foot blown off, but other than that, not so bad. Since Judas and Magdalene were considered the best fighter pilot robots, they were first in line for robot spare parts and were back in the fight within days.

So, it was really no surprise, considering Judas and Magdalene's stellar war record, that they were picked to fly Randy along with Michelangelo's cake from Rome to Hoboken. When they arrived there, Judas and Magdalene hovered their rocket plane, just like a lunar landing, onto the bomb-cratered parking lot of the Genesis Center. Greeted with a standing ovation from the robot staff of the center, Judas and Magdalene gave a thumbs-up. Randy, in turn, yelled into his robot controller, "Get back to work!"

Much like peaches and cream and biscuits and gravy, chocolate cake and white icing belong together. So, after Judas and Magdalene carried Michelangelo's cake into the Genesis Center dining hall, it was not surprising that Randy yelled into his robot controller, "Judas, you and Magdalene whip up some white icing!" Easier said than done: in this year of 2064, the only recipe for white icing called for a base of spare possum parts (lips, ears, and snouts). But after several trials, the robots managed to brew up an elixir that was not only white and spreadable, but also glowed in the dark.

"Lean your head back a little, Antonio," Judas asked.

"What the hell," Antonio replied.

"I want your neck to be clean as a whistle."

Despite not having a neck, or for that matter a face, Judas was giving Antonio a first-class shave, close but not bloody close. After scraping off the last whiskers from his neck, Judas found a clean towel and wiped the 100-year-old's soft and wrinkled face clean.

Meanwhile, down the hallway, in the Genesis Center dining hall, Randy was pacing back and forth in front of Antonio's 500-year-old birthday cake, while yelling into his robot controller, "Judas, where are you? Fox News has been waiting on you for the last ten minutes!"

Sifting through Antonio's dresser, Judas managed to find a clean and unripped T-shirt. Shaking out any obvious wrinkles with a snap of his wrist, Judas placed it over Antonio's head. "Stretch out your arms, Antonio." Pulling the shirt over his arms and down his chest, Judas whispered, "perfect fit." Wrapping his arms around and under Antonio, Judas gently lifted him into his wheelchair. Looking for a hairbrush, but settling for a ten-tooth comb, Judas brushed back Antonio's few strands of gray hair to the middle of his bald pate.

   "Antonio, I noticed you've got a 1970 boombox and a shoebox full of Beach Boys tapes. Here, why don't you put the boombox and the tapes on your lap and we can have a little music at your party?"

After placing the boombox and tapes on Antonio's lap, Judas stepped back and looked at the oldest Homo sapien left on earth. "You're looking good, Antonio. Got to look good—after all, this party will be your last hurrah."

"What the hell," Antonio replied.

By the time Judas had rolled Antonio into the Genesis dining hall, Magdalene and the house robots had not only spread the homemade white icing over Michelangelo's cake, but they had also placed a single candle on top of the masterpiece.

Having been a stand-up comedian in a previous life, the Master knew a thing or two about good timing. Just as Antonio was rolled over to his birthday cake, the Master appeared in the hall in the form of a hologram. Antonio, having never seen a hologram, gasped, "What the hell!"

"Hello, Antonio," the Master hologram said. "Congratulations on achieving your 100th birthday. What a remarkable moment for you.   And that wonderful chocolate cake baked by the great Michelangelo. I only wish that I could share a bite of that miraculous treat." Since the Master was at his retreat home at the South Pole, and he was right in the middle of a hot game of solitaire, he kept his remarks short. "So, enjoy your cake and your moment. Happy Birthday, Antonio!"

The assembled crowd, a mixture of robots, old sapiens, and Fox News toadies, applauded their fearless leader as his image faded from the hall. Judas walked over to the cake and lit the single candle. The crowd sang a short version of "Happy Birthday," and Antonio rolled himself over to his cousin's cake and blew out the candle without any commentary. Antonio grabbed a plastic fork from the mound of forks on the fork table. Judas flipped a Beach Boys tape into the boombox, and the boys began to sing, "God only knows what I'd be without you. "

With Fox News beaming out his every move to the entire world, Antonio dug into the chocolate cake, and just before he put the first bite into his mouth, he said, "What the hell!" When Antonio swallowed the first piece of the 500-year-old masterpiece, he instantly turned into dust.

A twenty-first century dominated by purple glow-in-the-dark possum parts, fake water, a desolate landscape, and mindless cartoons broadcast on a spineless TV network was no place to abide.

Even now, at this late date, the dreams of a twentieth century filled with colors, smells, tastes, and vibrant sounds swirled through the minds of the old humans at the Genesis Center— lazy summer days surrounded by green grass and trees, birds and critters, baseball games and skipping ropes, blue skies and white clouds overhead. It did not seem so long ago. All the sapiens of Genesis stumbled and walked over to Antonio's cake to get their fair share of this magical treat. It was, at last, their time to be released. With the Beach Boys singing "God only knows," the Sapiens of Genesis patiently waited in line for their turn to devour Michelangelo's marvelous gift. And so—poof, poof, poof—the humans of Genesis became dust.

The house robots, armed with brooms and dustpans, swept up the debris the home-grown humans had created, but a blizzard of refuse was brewing out in the Center's parking lot. Moon buggies, solo helicopters, and rocket hover planes were filling up the space around Genesis. The Fox News broadcast of

Antonio's party had inspired sapiens from around the globe to partake of their share of Michelangelo's chocolate cake. They came from the coldest places on earth: Alaska, Siberia, Iceland, Greenland, Canada, and Chicago. They came day and night, all standing in line waiting for their piece of the masterpiece. The piles of dust grew and grew, to the point that the robots had to start a compost heap in the backyard.

The bowl warmer, integrated into the arm of his La-Z-Boy chair, had always functioned without failure. So, when his bowl of SpaghettiOs became cold right in the middle of a game of Sonic the Hedgehog, the Master was irate. After his appearance at Antonio's birthday party, the Master had indulged himself with a routine of Pac-Man, Angry Bird, and Hedgehog video play time. Enabling the Master, his house robots supplied him with steaming-hot bowls of mouthwatering SpaghettiOs. Alas, the bowl warmer's malfunction threw the Master's routine into crisis. While he waited for the robots to rewire the warmer, the Master forced himself to watch Fox News. Coincidentally, the Fox News hosts were about to enjoy large slices of Michelangelo's cake. The Master had never had a reflective nature, but when he saw his constituents gobbling up Michelangelo's cake and turning to dust, he envisioned his empire going straight into the dust bin of history. The Master grabbed his hand-held robot controller and yelled, "Jeremiah, fire up the rocket plane—we are headed to Hoboken!"

 When they arrived at Genesis, the parking lot was filled with moon buggies, solo helicopters, and rocket planes, so Jeremiah, the Master's robot pilot, had to land 200 yards from the Center. Jumping out of the plane, the Master ran toward a long, serpentine line of his constituents and yelled, "Don't eat that cake! I promise SpaghettiOs for all! SpaghettiOs for all of you!"

Even if there were poets or dreamers left to lay claim to their imaginations, the presence of a constant cloudless tangerine sky would not be considered a benevolent space for inspiration or remembrance. The journey from remembrance to legend to myth can be long or short, depending on the foundational truth of the memories. Like dinosaurs or knights surrounding a round table, or a blue skyline dotted with meandering white clouds, or better—a thunderous lighting strike—these were, by 2064, considered sapiens myths. So, when a lightning bolt flashed out of a cloudless tangerine sky to strike the Master as he was running across the Genesis parking lot, it was as if a troop of knights had charged into the Genesis dining hall and tipped over a round table. A sapiens myth realized.

The two robots assigned to clean up the Master's ashes waited until the flames generated by the lighting strike abated. Using a couple of fireplace shovels and a hand broom, the robots scooped up the master's charred remains and dumped them on the compost heap in the backyard of Genesis.

Day after day, six days in all, the sapiens of the world made a pilgrimage to the Genesis Center to get their share of Michelangelo's cake. Finally, on the Saturday evening before Easter, our friend Randy was the last Homo sapiens left on the planet. Surrounded by robots and feeling abandoned, Randy handed his robot controller to Judas in exchange for a plastic fork. Judas, as he had told every other human before giving them a plastic fork, said, "Be sure to get lots of icing on your fork."

Scooping up a good-sized piece of cake, Randy turned to Judas and said, "Until we meet again." And then—poof—Randy was dust.

Judas turned on the robot controller and pushed the All button, which alerted all the robots of the world. Judas, imitating

Randy, put the controller up to his globular head and yelled, "To all robots near and far, free the possums from their cages!" So it was that all the imprisoned possums were released from their cages to live out their lives as they were meant to be—in freedom.

After flipping another Beach Boys tape into Antonio's boombox, Judas walked over to Magdalene. After giving her a fist bump, they began to snap their fingers to the slow rhythm of the music. As the beat picked up steam, Judas and Magdalene started to tap their toes, shimmy their shoulders, sway their hips, and then promenade across the Genesis dining hall. And when the Beach Boys belted out the signature lines of their song, the house robots began to clap just as Judas and Magdalene spun their globular heads around as the boys sang, "Good, good, good, good vibrations!"

As Easter dawned, the sun's ascension flushed the darkness from the heavens, and its flickering light exposed a barren landscape.

And it was good.

An apparition, a dark bellowing cloud, descended from the crystal tangerine sky.

And it was good.

 Energized by lightning bolts, the ever-darkening cloud proliferated across the horizon.

And it was good.

Pregnant with moisture, the darkening cloud boiled with intent.

And it was good.

Bursting with life, the cloud showered rain upon a parched earth.

And it was good.

In the wink of an eternal eye, the fields, pastures, and forests sprang back to life. And the lakes, rivers, and streams flowed with clean water again.

And it was good.

As seen from heaven, as on earth, the planet grew green and splashed blue again.

And it was good.

Framed by the stars, the third planet from the sun was once again speckled with the colors of the spectrum displayed on a canvas of green and blue. Resurrected, the earth was once again a masterpiece.   And it was very good.

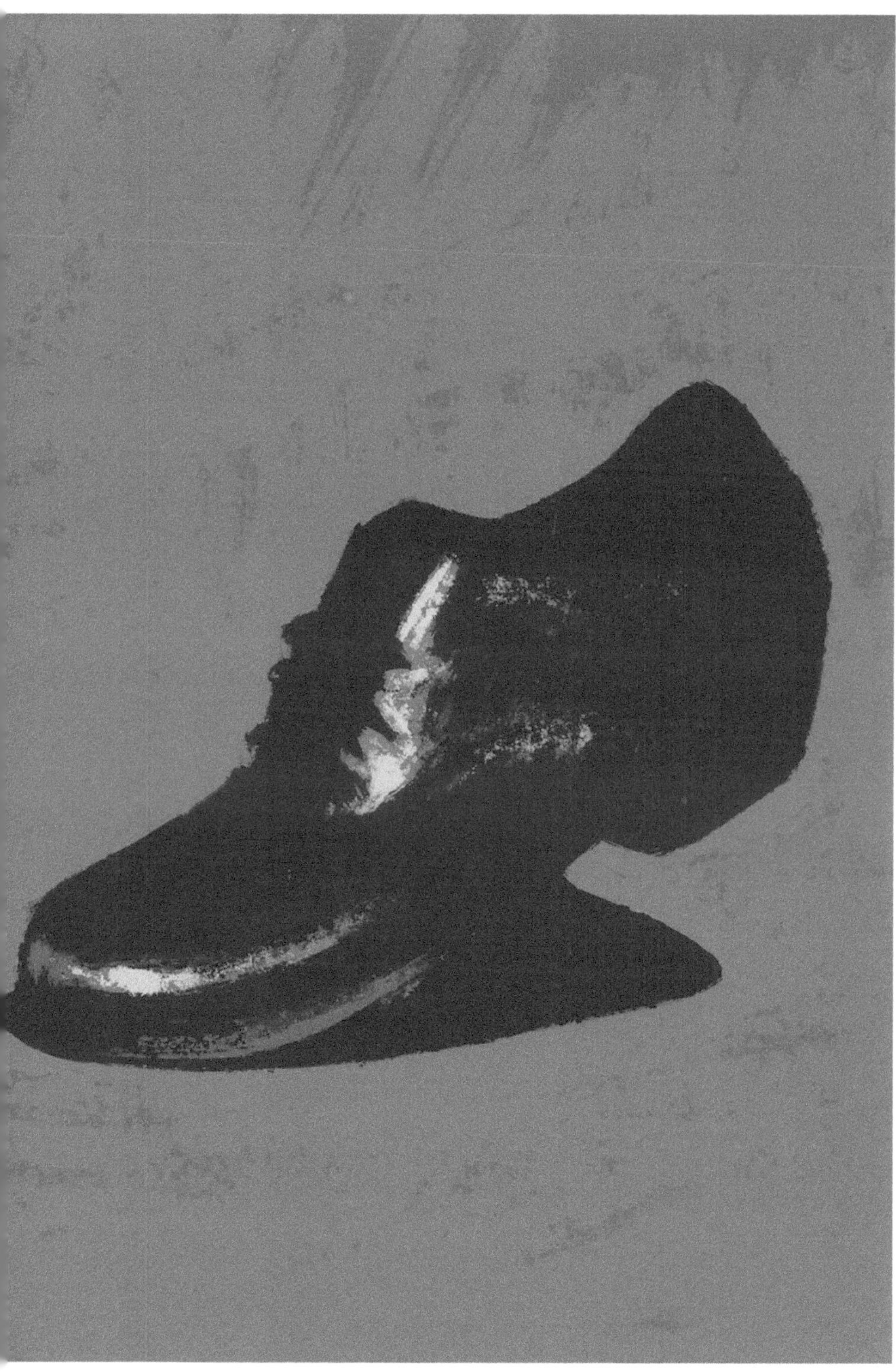

Silence

The windowless cinder blocked hallway and the low-slung snapping fluorescent lights did not flatter the gatekeeper's appearance, but his black dyed mustache and dark red lips did highlight his pale complexion. Dressed in gray fatigues, a frayed brown leather shoulder belt, and a silver peaked cap, the keeper stood sentry in front of the locked double-doored entrance to Studio B.

Perhaps thousands of years from now, Archeologists will sift through our ruins and dig up a limestone block with the word-STUDIO-B-chiseled onto its face and they will debate the meaning of such. But, for the fifteen pedestrians, twelve nuns, eight Romanians, and the two elites rummaging at the entrance to Studio-B, the limestone etching- "Studio-B"- above the double doored entrance meant that this was the home of "Ted's Amateur Radio Half-Hour". Before releasing this group into Studio-B, the keeper had some important matters to address. Stepping up upon the third step of a three stepladder, the keeper pointed toward the locked double-door.

"Before you pass over to the other side, you must be attuned to Ted's Ten Commandments."

Waving a yellowish parchment above his head, the keeper continued his preachment-

"Number one- You must obey the instructions flashed on the sign located at the rear of the stage.

Number two- No stomping of your feet.

Number three-No standing on your seats.

Number four- No drinking pop or booze or water.

Number five-No chewing of food or gum or candy or tobacco.

Number six-No weapons allowed-not even pistols.

Number seven-No coughing or spitting or belching or farting or

Talking.

Number eight-No sex-legal or otherwise.

Number nine-No smoking cigarettes or cigars or marijuana.

Number ten- Compliance of these Commandments is not negotiable."

The Keeper stopped to point at himself, "And I will enforce such!"

Once released into Studio-B, the twelve nuns from "Daughters of the Lamb Orphanage "trotted fast enough to claim all the front row seats before the selfish people got them. There were no stained-glass windows or even kneelers in Studio-B, but once the rest of the rabble found their seats and silence reigned; the nuns felt right at home. With the familiar sounds of the pitter-patter of scurrying rodents under foot, the nuns felt that they were knee-deep into those golden silent moments just before their formal routine prayers of Vespers or the 9th Hour. Their moment was interrupted by the start of Ted's theme song, "Roll Out the Barrel." Emerging from behind the curtains, Ted, despite his size, swayed to the music, and moved to the darkest corner of the stage.

The neon sign at the back of the stage flashed – Applause.

The audience clapped.

Standing on a pedestal behind Ted, the show's model was dressed in a snow-white evening gown, high heels, fire engine red lipstick, raccoon grade eye shadow, and a perpetual toothy grin. She also had a two-handed grip of the flashing neon signs on and off clicker.

Soon after Ted rattled down into his overstuffed recliner, the week's three contestants, unhindered by leg irons, shuffled out from behind the curtains. As the music continued to blast and the flashing neon sign's instructions ricocheting off their backs, the contestants marched, in lock step, to their designated spots at the front of the stage.

Once the music stopped and the neon sign went blank, the audience observed silence. Only then did the keeper station himself in front of the only exit.

The weight of a full tumbler of Jack Daniels and the three stacks of 3X5 index cards challenged the stability of Ted's worn-out card table. Fortuitously, the table was propped up against Ted's recliner and any wobbles that Ted managed to contrive were absorbed. After a two- gulp swig from his tumbler, Ted encroached upon the silence of Studio-B, by yelling out to his audience. "Welcome Ladies and Gents to Ted's Armature Radio Half-Hour! "

The sign flashed Applause! The audience clapped.

The sign went blank. The audience observed silence.

"Our first contestant tonight is Mindy, a ten-year-old from the Upper Eastside of Manhattan. For all of you out there in radioland, little Mindy is all dressed up in a costume that looks like it's laced with diamonds. By golly, she looks like real rich britches."

The Sign flashed- laugh! the audience laughed.

The sign went blank. The audience observed silence.

Ted reached over to grab the first stack of 3X5 index cards. "My 3X5 card says that Mindy's parents, the two elitists' sitting by themselves in the last row of Studio-B has been dolling out outrageous amounts of money to teach Mindy how to tap dance. Is that right, Mindy?"

"Yes." Said Mindy.

Ted flipped to his next index card. "The card says you will dance your heart out tonight, but you will come in second place." Ted flipped to the next card. "The card says when you get home tonight that your parents will throw away your ruby red tap shoes and give away your cute diamond studded costume to Goodwill. And their two- word critique of your performance tonight will be simple enough- 'Not Worthy'." Ted flipped to his next 3X5 card- "And so, it will be for the rest of your life Mindy, that your elite schoolteachers, hoity-toity husband, smarty-pants children and your snobby interior decorator, will all consider you-Not Worthy." Ted flipped to Mindy's last card. "So, at the end of your life, when you're starring out of your Nursing Home bedroom window at the illegal immigrants mowing the plush lawn and gardening the shinning beds of flowers, you will look back to this moment, to this very moment, here at Ted's Half-hour, and know this was the highlight of your life." Ted threw Mindy's cards in a near-by trash can. "Without further ado-here's Mindy tap dancing to the pleasant enough melody of Eastside-Westside."

The Sign Flashed-Applause! The audience clapped.

The sign went blank. The audience observed silence.

 The day after Mindy's Mother had seen Shirley Temple tap dance with Bojangles in "The Little Colonel "she signed her daughter up for tap dancing lessons-Mindy was three years old. By the time Mindy took the stage at Studio-B, she had been tapping for seven years, so when the music of "Eastside-Westside" began, Mindy stepped right into a time step tap. She followed with a brush slide and then a drag with her left tap shoe. Mindy twirled, waved, and smiled as she tapped across the stage. She tapped around Ted and his recliner, she tapped off the show model's pedestal and as the music reached a crescendo, Mindy shimmied her way for a stage left exit.

 The Sign Flashed-Applause! The audience clapped.

 The sign went blank. The audience observed silence.

Just after taking another gulp of Jack Daniels, Ted reached for the next stack of 3X5 index cards. Ted flipped to the first card. "Alrighty then, our next contestant is Cristian, an illegal immigrant from Romania. "

The sign flashed- Applause! The audience clapped.

 The sign went blank. The audience observed silence.

  "Cristian has an eight-person fan club setting right here in Studio-B. For all of you out there in Radioland, they look like a motley crew. They all look like dirty no-good Gypsies to me, and I am sure they are illegal immigrants too."

The sign flashed- BOO! The Audience- BOOED.

The sign went blank. The Audience observed Silence.

"My index card tells me that you're going to sing the Romanian folksong, Mia-Dorule. Is that right Cristian?"

"Da!" Cristian answered.

"My 3X5 card also says you will accompany yourself with a Hurdy-Gurdy. Is that right?"

"Da"

"My 3X5 says you will be booed off the stage tonight."

Pointing to the keeper at the rear of Studio-B, Ted continued-

"Our keeper will handcuff you as soon as you finish your song and lead you out to the hallway, where two Federal agents await. The index card says you will be deported back to Romania, and you will be arrested as soon as you get off the plane. You will spend the next 43 years of your life in jail. You will finally be released in 1990, when the Communist Government falls. Then you will spend the rest of your days, playing your Hurdy-Gurdy and singing awful Romanian folksongs on the street corners of Bucharest, begging for money."

"Da" said Cristian.

"So, without further ado, here's Cristian playing his Hurdy-Gurdy and singing Mia-Dorule."

Cristian played his heart out, but his voice was shaky, and his Hurdy-Gurdy was out of tune. So, when he finally finished-

The sign flashed- BOO! The audience BOOED.

The sign went blank. The audience observed silence.

As luck would have it, Cristian had strapped his Hurdy-Gurdy around his neck. So, when the keeper greeted him with handcuffs, as he left the stage, he was able to take his instrument back to his beloved Romania. So, for the next 43 years he was able to torment his cellmates with his out of tune Hurdy-Gurdy.

 Just after scooping up the last stack of 3X5 index cards, Ted, yelled out to the crowd in Studio-B and to his audience in radioland-

 "Ladies and Gents, this here will be hard to believe, but we got ourselves a genuine bone-a fide orphan as our last contestant tonight! Izzy by name-orphan by trade and he has a twelve-member fan club too!"

 Pointing down at the front row of seats, Ted observed-

 "For all of you out there in radioland, we got a whole row of nuns here in Studio-B. Looks like a herd of Penguins to me."

The sign flashed - laugh. The audience laughed.

The sign went dark. The audience observed silence.

 "So, Izzy your first 3x5 card says you were trained to sing and play guitar by the head nun of Daughters of the Lamb Orphanage, Mary-Margret. Where is she sitting?"

 "Yes, Ted, Mother Superior Mary-Margret is my teacher, my mentor, she is my muse. And she is sitting in the first seat in the front row, with her head bowed in prayer."

 Ted looked down on Mary-Margret- "So, what you are praying about Sister?"

 Looking up at Ted and then glancing at the dark sign, Mary-Margret did not respond.

 "Are you hard of hearing? What are you praying about?!"

The sign flashed- Stand up Sister and speak.

 Mary-Margret stood up and pointed her finger at Ted.

"Ted, I was observing a moment of silence for Izzy. Not unlike the silence we observe just before Vespers or the 9th Hour of Prayer. It is a silence earned from listing to your soul. And I'm wishing for Izzy to do the absolute best that he can and maybe his dreams will come true."

Ted straightened himself in his recliner and then choked down a slug of Jack Daniel's. He pointed his finger at Mary-Margret and said-

"Be careful Mary-Margret, what you wish for, it just might come true."

Mary-Margret's life was one of routine prayer, orphanage responsibilities, tip-toed gaits, and silence. But if the truth is told, Mary-Margret also took time for wishful dreaming. Each evening, just after Compline (the final formal prayer of the day) she would tip-toe her way through the maze of hallways to her office for a few solitary moments before Izzy came rapping at her door for his daily music lesson. In those few moments Mary-Margret would dream of Izzy's musical future. Maybe, just maybe he will become a star, and maybe he will be so grateful to her, that he will give back to the Orphanage and maybe they could afford new padded kneelers for the sanctuary or have enough to fix the stained-glass window in the church or even have a few dollars left over for her to be treated to a Friday evening meal of finely whipped potatoes, crisp green beans with almonds shaved on top, and maybe even a grilled salmon drenched in virgin Greek olive oil and sprinkled with exotic herbs from faraway Morocco. Invariably, Mary Margret's dreams plunged back to reality when Izzy came knocking on her door.

Ted flipped to the next 3X5 index card.

"Izzy your card says you are going to sing one of my favorites- Jiminy Cricket's classic song- 'When you wish upon a star'."

"Yes, Ted, and I'm going to accompany myself with my six-string guitar."

 Flipping to the next card, Ted continued-

"And the card says you will sing Jiminy's song almost as well as Jiminy himself. And you will easily win the contest tonight."

 "That's wonderful Ted."

Ted flipped to the next 3X5 index- "The card says that there is a record executive sitting among the pedestrians in the audience tonight and he will be so impressed with your applause-o-meter number, that he will sign you to a million-dollar contract right after the show."

 "I'm really getting excited."

Flipping to yet another card- "The card says you will become incredibly famous and, in the years ahead. You will even appear on the Ed Sullivan television show. "

"What's television?"

 Pointing down at the Mary-Margret Ted continued- "And Izzy, you will have no time or money for your muse over there, Mary-Margret. So, I guess the old head nun will just be out of luck, hope and dreams. So, how do like them apples Mary-Margret?"

 Mary-Margret stood up and pointed her finger at Ted. "Ted you are nothing more than a barstool bully and you preach nothing but hatred." she replied, "And your loud superficial bullying is a product of anger deep inside your soul. You might want to try some reflective silence."

The sign flashed-sit down Mary-Margret and shut up!

Mary-Margret sat down in silence.

Ted flipped to the next card- "Izzy you will spend a lifetime singing sappy Disney songs to the very young and the incredibly old."

"Sounds wonderful."

And then Ted flipped to the last 3x5 card- "This card says you will die at age 110, in the arms of your twenty-three-year-old seventh wife. There will be a grand funeral for you at the National Cathedral and the President of the United States will give the eulogy. And there will be a statue of you and Jiminy Cricket built on the front lawn of the White House."

"Can't wait."

"So, without further a-do it my pleasure and honor to introduce America to their newest icon-Izzy, singing one of the greatest songs in American history- 'When you wish upon a star'."

The sign flashed – Applaud.

The Audience-Clapped. (except for the nuns, who sat in silence)

The sign- Went blank.

The Audience-Observed Silence

If you closed your eyes, you would swear that Jiminy himself was singing. By the time he got to the climax of the song--- "anything your heart desires will come true"- there were many in the audience holding back their tears.

The sign flashed-Stand up and Applaud

The Audience-Stood up and clapped. (The nuns remained silent with their arms folded in front of them.)

The sign went blank.

The Audience-Sat back in their seats and observed silence.

For the first time in the ten-year history of his show, Ted got up from his recliner after a performance.

"Ladies and Gents," Ted's voice began to quiver, "Jiminy would have" Ted stopped to steady himself, "Jiminy would have loved that rendition."

The sign flashed – applaud.

The Audience – clapped. (Except for the nuns.)

The sign-Went Blank

The Audience – Observed Silence

By the time Ted waddled back to his recliner and oozed himself back down into it, the show's model had dragged Mindy and the Applause-O-Meter out to join Izzy at center stage.

"Alrighty then!' Ted yelled, "Now comes the moment for truth!"

In the ten-year history of Ted's show, plate spinning acts were always extremely popular. So, it really was no surprise that just last week, "Jimmy the Stewart-the magical spinning savant", had set the Applause-o-Meter record for the show, with a 9.6 reading.

"Are you capable of besting Jimmy's 9.6 reading?" Ted challenged, "I think not!"

Ultimately, it really did not make any difference since the preordained was going to be ordained- record or not.

"First up for your judgement is cute little Mindy-the tap-dancing elite!"

Ted waved his hand toward the back of Studio-B.

"Keeper! Dim the lights!"

Except for the flickering light of the Applause-o-Meter, Studio-B went dark.

"And flip on the spotlight!"

Mindy's knees buckled under the weight of the light. Her manicured skin was whitewashed by the glare of the light and her ruby red tap shoes were hidden in the shadows. But Mindy's diamond clustered custom rainbowed a spectrum of colors that dazzled the audience. Even Ted yelped out loud- "Well-Hello!"

"So, without further ado – let's give it up for the rich kid!"

The sign flashed- Applause – but not too much

The Audience-Clapped and Clapped.

The Applause-o-Meter's needle began to rise- 8.0-8.5-8.6

Other than the Meter and the spotlight, Studio-B was bathed in darkness, so it was not known who the first person was to start stomping their feet, but the betting money was on Sister Mary-Constance. The rest of the nuns began stomping their feet too.

The needle started to go higher. 8.7-8.8-8.9 9.0

The sign flashed- Sisters! You're desecrating the 1st and 2nd Commandments!

The Meter continued to rise-9.2 then 9.4 then 9.5 then 9.6

The sign flashed- Keeper! Stop them! Stop them!

But, by the time the keeper settled the nuns down, the damage was done. Mindy had the new Applause-o-Meter record- 9.7

The sign – Went Blank

The Audience-Observed Silence

When the house lights were turned back on and the spotlight dimmed, the show's model was sitting on the edge of her pedestal. Her hairpiece had gravitated down her forehead and her toothy grin had become a sour smirk, but she still had a two-handed grip of the sign's clicker. And just before licking out the bottom of his glass tumbler with his extra-long tongue, Ted had drained what was left of his Jack Daniel's.

"Alrighty then!" Ted yelled, "Ladies and Gents we got some damage to control! Keeper! Dim the lights! And flick on the spotlight!"

Blinded by the spotlight, Izzy instinctively put his hand up to shade himself from the glare.

"So, without further a-do, let's hear it for the rightful winner- Izzy!"

The sign flashed- Stand up and cheer-shout and yell.

The Audience-Stood and clapped and cheered. The nuns sat in silence.

The Applause-O-Meter went up to 7.0 then 7.5 then 8.0

The sign flashed-Louder! Louder! Stand up-You too Sisters!

Mary-Constance was the first nun to stand. Even though she was burdened by her habit, she still managed to get up on her chair, shake her fist in the air and yell- "BOOOOOO! BOOOOO!" Soon enough, the other Sisters followed. One after another, they stood up on their seats and shook their fists and yelled – BOOOOO! BOOOOO!

The sign flashed- Sisters! You are violating the 3rd Commandment! There will be consciousness for your disobedience! I demand you sit down and observe silence.

The Meter's needle inched up to 8.5 then 9.0 then 9.5 then to 9.6

Mother Superior Mary-Margret was the last Sister to stand. Age and gumption contributed to her not standing up on her chair, but the urge to follow her minions' lead did cross her mind. She gazed up at the spotlighted image of Izzy. His blond hair had turned to white, and his pimpled face had become a death masked version of a healthy twenty-year-old. Mary-Margret reached her arm out to Izzy and in turn Izzy turned his face away from his lifelong mentor. Mary-Margret-the teacher-the mentor-the muse, raised her fist up and out in a fit of anger screamed -

"Boo! I say, Boo!"

The Applause-O-Meter's needle hit 9.8 and Izzy not only won the contest, but he also signed a million-dollar contract and immediately left on a 100-stop concert tour. As was foreseen by Ted's prophecy he made tons of money and did not give Mary - Margret or the orphanage a single penny.

There would be no padded kneelers, or repaired stain glass windows, no whipped mash potatoes, green beans and no grilled salmon drenched in virgin Greek olive oil sprinkled with exotic herbs from faraway Morocco. No, all that was left for Mary-Margret was routine prayers, orphanage responsibilities, tip-toed gaits and silence.

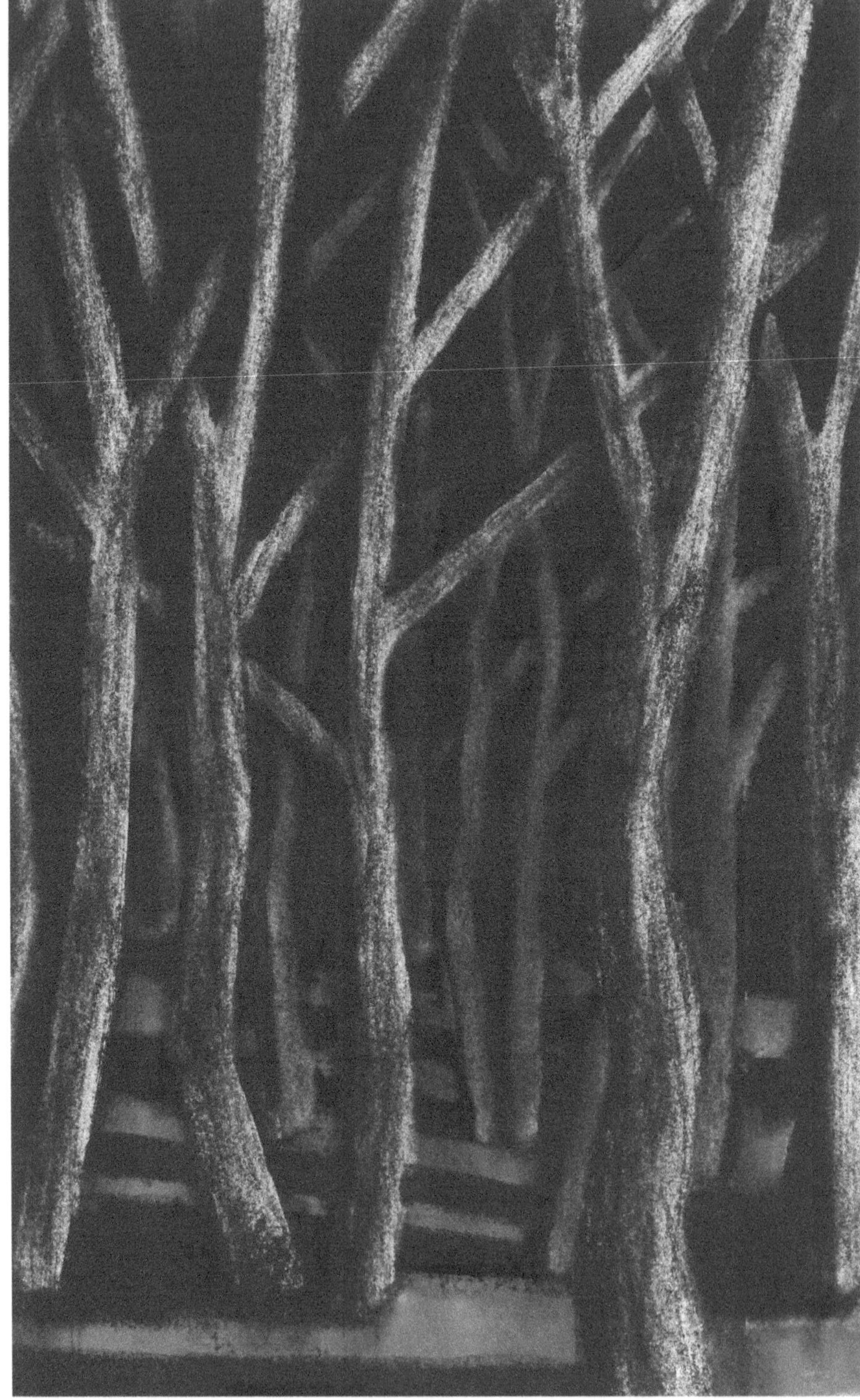

Shadow Ridge

 The sugar maple, river birch, white ash, yellow poplar, and oak trees that edged Stumble Road, an old log trail, were so thick that they formed a shadowy canopy, forcing Sheriff Jacob to flick on the headlights of his squad car. The three-mile journey up Shadow Ridge, to Papa-Daddy's cabin, took way too much time for an ordinary person and twice the same for an impatient Sheriff. Expecting to see Papa's cabin around the next bend or twist in the road, the Sheriff was repeatedly disappointed. Stumble Road was the only road up Shadow Ridge and it dead-ended at the front porch of Papa-Daddy's cabin.

 Prison walls are grayer, but the wall of trees that surrounded Pappy-Daddy's homestead produced a purple shadow that swallowed the daylight from the sky. Stepping over a threshold of wild marigolds and fresh weeds, Papa and his only child, Alfie, penetrated the woods. Encased within the wall of trees was a grand old oak tree, and upon the biggest and lowest branch, Papa had constructed a sturdy deer stand, which was made from the finest teak wood and carefully molded and shaped to withstand any human folly or even nature's wrath. Standing at the base of the oak tree, Papa offered his son his hand and together they ascended a homemade ladder up onto Papa's stand. This being Alfie's 10th birthday, Papa thought it was about time for his first kill. Alfie had seen and felt death, but never of his own making. Shouldering a past birthday gift, a British 1938 Parker-Hale sniper rifle, which he had nicknamed *Parkie*, Alfie laid out in a prone position across the deer stand and took aim at a tree bourn squirrel and with a single squeeze of the trigger ended the life of a robust, and contented critter. One of the two squirrels came crashing to the forest's floor, fatal wound intact. Father and son descended from the deer stand to the forest, stepping over and around the undergrowth. Settling into a squat next to Alfie's kill, Papa waved his son to his side. Papa gently grabbed Alfie's right hand and pulled him down for a closer inspection. Separating out his index finger from the others, he placed Alfie's finger into the fatal wound. He then traced Alfie's finger up to his forehead. Alfie tried to wipe away the still warm blood from his head, but Papa pulled his hand away and gently whispered- "Easy-Peezy,"

 The chattering of the surviving squirrel echoed across the dense forest, but it was not loud enough to drown out the distant sound of a car churning its way up Shadow Ridge. Papa grabbed his son's hand with his left hand and the dead squirrel's tail with his right hand and they ran back to the safety of their cabin, which was a mere stone's throw away.

By the time Sheriff Jacob came to a jolting halt right behind Papa's 1946 Dodge 6-wheeled Power wagon pick-up, the surviving squirrel had abandoned his chattered protest and moved deeper into the bowels of the darkened forest. After maneuvering his belly past the steering wheel, the Sheriff struggled to open the squad car's rusted door. The muddy ruts that surrounded Papa's homestead provided a balance obstacle that Jacob solved by using the side panels of Papa's pick-up as a crutch. As he staggered toward the front porch of the cabin, the Sheriff gently patted the panel, but then he slid his hand along the scraps and dents of the bed of the truck. Giving into his instincts, Jacob licked the palm of his hand. Cornmeal and sugar were certain to meet on rare occasions and then only not for legal, but that is what Jacob's sensitive taste buds revealed. Looking back at the bed of the pick-up the Sheriff added a funny look to his usual stoic demeanor. The sheriff managed to notice more than the empty cans of rifle lubricant scattered across the sagging front porch of the cabin. The red "No Trespassing" painted on the steel front door caught his eye as well. The creaking of the front steps confirmed their warped appearance, and that Jacob probably needed to lose a few pounds. Once on the porch, the good Sheriff reached into his pocket and unfolded his search warrant. Looking straight into the "No" of the "No Trespassing" sign, Jacob yelled out-

"Search warrant, Papa -Daddy, I got a warrant!"

Leaning his good ear toward the steel door, Jacob heard nothing.

"Search warrant!" he repeated.

He leaned closer. Nothing but silence.

"Papa? Papa, I know you there!"

With a backyard of talkative hens, and a noisy rooster too, Jacob was not accustomed to silence, especially the silence of an accused moonshiner. He moved his ear away from the door and stepped back as quietly as the sagging porch aloud. The Sheriff kept his left hand wrapped around the warrant, but he slid his right hand down to his service revolver.

"Papa?" he whispered.

Jacob gripped his pistol and flicked off the safety with his thumb.

'Papa?" he repeated.

Perhaps Jacob had seen one too many Westerns, but when he heard the first bolt being released, he drew his pistol out of his holster just like he had seen a thousand times on TV. After the last of the three bolts locking the steel door had been released, Papa creaked the door open. Looking down at the Sheriff's drawn pistol, Papa whispered, "Easy—Peezy."

The dim light, emitted from a rose- colored kerosene lamp, placed at the center of the pine-tared picnic table in the middle of the front room, was the only source of light. The fragrance of a three-day- old pot of squirrel gravy, and a pan of grease fried turtle parts resting on a rusted wood burning stove detracted the Sheriff from his critique of the room's décor. The two World War II cots in the corner of the kitchen were noticed by Jacob, especially the cot occupied by Papa's son. Alfie's lack of a smile was not too surprising considering the sobriety of the occasion. Cradling his *Parkie* in his left hand, Alfie held up his right hand, spreading his fingers out to shield himself from the kerosene lamp's beam of light. The shadow that graced his squinted face managed to conceal any embarrassment or sorrow that Jacob had hoped to detect. The sight of a fresh urine stain on the front of the boy's britches backed the Sheriff away from the corner of the room. Pointing to Alfie's plight he looked back at Papa and asked-

 "What's wrong with the little feller?"

"Excitable." Papa said "Excitable."

  By this time in the search, Jacob felt safe enough to put his pistol back in his holster and he placed the search warrant on the picnic table. Having seen and smelled enough of the front room Jacob asked if there was another room to search. Papa pointed down a dark hallway to what he called Arsenal. Papa opened a sturdy door and flicked on the lights to a large room. The chandeliers that lined the ceiling were a good match for the white marble floor and the windowless walnut paneled walls. The oak hand-crafted tables that lined the room were certainly sturdy enough to hold the arsenal of weapons that the room's name implied. Pointing toward the stacks of weapons piled upon the tables Jacob asked if he would be allowed to "touch the booty. "

"Yes," Papa replied, "but for God's sake take off those muddy boots."

Jacob's socks were yellow from sweat and mud, but Papa was generous enough to overlook the soured nature of Jacob's stocking feet.

The first table within reach, had all the best knives and swords available from the known Civilized world. There were boot and neck knives, bayonets and combat tomahawks too. There were two Prussian sabers, and three Imperial Navy swords, along with a stack of World War II Japanese Shin-gunto swords. The very next table was even better. Papa had gathered some of the best war making pistols of all time. He had everything from several two-shot derringers to 6 Colt 45's to a 1900 Browning to a British flintlock, and of course, a large stack of Ceska 38's. Even though the rifle table did have a World War II M-1 and a Springfield from WWI, Jacob only fondled the Whitworth sniper rifle. Even though the corner table had just three bazookas and only one Laneiafiammse flamethrower, the display was fortified by several milk crates filled to the brim with all manner of hand grenades, but the next table tugged on Jacob's heart. Barely containing himself he rushed over to the machine gun table. Right on top of the heap of guns was a fully loaded 1926 Tommy Gun. It was not too much of a stretch to imagine Al Capone cleaning and lubricating the various moving parts of the gun. Jacob cradled it in his arms and held it up to his belly, but just as he began to rock back and forth, Papa turned on the spotlight in the middle of the room and there, sitting atop a tripod, on a hand-crafted walnut pedestal, was a World War II .50 caliber machine gun. Jacob quickly placed the Tommy gun back in its place and turned toward the center of the room. Unaware or maybe very aware, Jacob added a John Wayne swagger to his gait, as he shuttled his way toward the 50-cal.

Each of us has had moments in our lives that stand above our routine. Special moments that pass the test of fading memory. Moments that can even follow us to a nursing home and even to your death bed mumblings. Moments told so often that they graduate to the status of stories and maybe even penetrate your eulogy. Jacob had accumulated a few of those moments in his life. There was the time, as a six-year-old, that he fired his first rifle, killing a bunny in his backyard. Or the time, years later, when he finally won the mud wrestling contest over Trixie and Dixie, the middle-aged strippers at *Auntie Em's Lunch Buffet and Strip Bar Emporium*. And, of course, the pride he felt when he ushered in ten hens and one rooster into his homemade chicken coop in his backyard. But, with the spotlight's beam sparkling off the 45-inch barrel of the 50-cal, this moment was to go beyond any story told or eulogy given. This very moment, this spine-tingling moment, was now a thing of legend.

Jacob's hand quivered above the trigger of the machine gun, but he allowed his fingers to touch the lubricated flesh of the 45-inch barrel. He stroked his fingers across -back and forth, back and forth. It was in the middle of his fourth stroke that he felt a familiar warmth between his legs. He had no time to spare, Jacob reluctantly pulled his fingers off the barrel and headed for the exit. Keeping his eyes on the marbled floor, Jacob grabbed his boots and ran out of Papa-Daddy's cabin and scrambled through the mud to his squad car. He ripped open the rusted door and squeezed his stomach around and over the steering wheel. Jacob wheeled away from Papa-Daddy's cabin and back down Shadow Ridge. Once he got out from under the canopy of trees, Jacob allowed himself to look down at his britches. The fresh urine stain was barely noticeable and the pungent smell barely penetrated Jacob's senses. As he pulled out onto the highway and 60-mph flow, it was abundantly clear to Jacob that the little feller and he had one thing in common-they were both- excitable. In the panic of leaving the cabin Jacob had left behind the search warrant and any questions he could have asked Alfie. The little feller could have told him about all the people that came and went all hours of the day and night, that there was a large moonshine still in the backyard and there was a sawed-off shotgun behind the steel front door. But Jacob was sure of one thing, the next time he went up Shadow Ridge, he was not going to retreat down the Ridge without a substantial booty.

Sometimes, when Alfie adjusted his body to accommodate his Parkie, his cot would moan in response, but the smooth stock and cool barrel rubbing up against his face compensated for any discomfort he might feel from his World War II bedding. Papa generally left the kerosene lamp burning through the night and into daylight, so that when Alfie woke up in the morning the flickering lamp was his dawn's light. But, on this night, any discomfort or flickering lamp was interrupted by the roar of a car's engine and the brilliance of headlights shining into the cabin's front room. Papa got up from his cot, put on his britches and tip-toed toward their steel door. Just after he picked up his sawed-off shotgun, Papa took a good listening posture, leaning into the front door. The front steps creaked and the porch too. And then Alfie and Papa clearly heard from just beyond the front door-

"Papa—you come out-with your hands up!   You hear? "

Cradling his shotgun in his left arm and hand, Papa unlocked the bolts that held the steel door in place and with each turn of a lock Papa whispered- "Easy-Peezy."

Embracing his *Parkie*, Alfie lay still in his cot, even after he saw the flash and heard the pop of the Sheriff's pistol and the thud of his Daddy's body slamming up against their steel door. Even the creaking footsteps and the wagging flashlight beam heading toward Arsenal did not tempt Alfie to abandon his urine-soaked cocoon. The slugo gait that Jacob achieved as he paraded back and forth between the Arsenal and Papa's Power-Wagon pick-up was predictable and the moans and groans of this middle-aged fatso of a man were too. Even in the coolness of the pre-dawn, Jacob was soaked in sweat by the time he had loaded all the weapons from the Arsenal into the bay of the Power-Wagon. Pivoting his path, Jacob tip-toed his way around the edge of the picnic table. Starring down on the boy's situation, Jacob pointed his pistol toward Alfie's head and commanded-

"Give me the rifle."

 Alfie, unrehearsed for such a moment, held onto his Parkie and simply replied – "No."

Yes, Jacob was a fatso, but he was a strong fatso. "OK then." he said, as he reached down and swept up the cot, Parkie, and Alfie too. He carried them around the picnic table, and out to the sagging front porch and down the creaking front steps to the Power Wagon, where he threw them on top of all the other weapons. Despite the comfort of Parkie, the gravity of the situation and the cool air gave Alfie a shiver that penetrated all the way through his urine-stained britches. Even after Jacob threw the still warm Laneiafiammse flamethrower into the back of the pick-up, Alfie could not control his shaking. Perhaps the flamethrower was not hot enough to comfort the little feller, since Jacob only used it to burn down the cabin, flame his squad car and torch the moonshine still. Only after the bumpy journey back down Shadow Ridge and the unloading of all the weapons into Jacob's remote barn on route 372, was Alfie able to calm down enough to talk.

"Where's Papa?" Alfie asked

"Burnt to a crisp." Jacob replied.

As he turned his back on Alfie, the Sheriff had the swagger of a man who had all his ducks in a row. After all, he had burnt up all the evidence, stowed away all the weapons, and had arranged to have Alfie placed in the "Orphanage for the Criminally Insane and the Destitute." What could possibly go wrong. No one would ever believe the story of an illiterate 10-year-old bedwetter. Yes, he had thought of everything, except to check if Alfie had a live round in the chamber of his rifle. As the Sheriff skipped his way toward the 50-cal in the corner of the barn, Alfie got up from his cot and as he had done so many times before, he cocked his one single round into the firing chamber of his 1938 Parker-Hale sniper rifle, he placed the wooden stock into the round of his shoulder and aimed his weapon straight at the sweaty back of the Sheriff and just before he squeezed the trigger of his weapon he softly whispered to himself- "Easy Peezy "

Not only was Jacob a fatso, but he was also clumsy too. So, just as Alfie fired his rifle, Jacob tripped over Al Capone's tommy gun. Alfie missed, and just as Jacob had predicted, no one believed Alfie's version of the Shadow Ridge Saga. Alfie was sent off to the Orphanage and the grateful citizens of the County gave the Sheriff a hero's parade for his brave stand against that "evil moonshiner" up on Shadow Ridge.

By 1966, Alfie had spent eight years confined to the "Orphanage for the Criminally Insane and the Destitute". Eight years of sleeping on a urine-stained cot in an unheated cell, surrounded by rodents, cockroaches, and weirdoes. Eight years of embracing his only friend-retribution. On his 18th birthday a County Judge gave Alfie a break.

"You can leave this institution if you enlist in the Army and go on a straight line to the war in Vietnam."   The Judge said.

So it was, Alfie left the Orphanage and went on a straight- line to the Army's basic training at Fort Leonard Wood, Missouri. Not long after basic training ended, but before deployment to Vietnam, Alfie made a visit to route 372. Lumpy from age and graveled on purpose, Route 372 was on a straight-line to Sherriff Jacob's barn. Between the road and a sea of corn, the old barn sagged from rot and disrepair. The double -wide doors were pad locked, but Alfie found a big rock and broke the lock with straight -line blows. Swatting away spiders and their webs, Alfie managed to find his rifle right where he had left it eight years ago. As luck would have it, the Laneiafiamma flamethrower was sitting on a table right next to his rifle. Just before Alfie fired up the flamethrower and torched the barn, he whispered to himself- "Easy-Peezy."

So it was, all the rifles, pistols, swords, knives, tommy guns, bazookas, even the 50 cal—all his father's legacy, save for the 1938 Parker-Hale sniper rifle, were burnt to a crisp. With Parkie slung over his shoulder Alfie walked away from the burning and exploding barn. Alfie felt the warm embrace of retribution, but as Alfie walked on a straight-line to fight in Vietnam, he would soon find out that retribution, which is birthed by anger, is the child of hate.

Hugo and Victor

An overnight rain had masked the aroma of the dog and pony manure that encircled the circus compound, and a crisscrossed web of filled clotheslines stretching across the compound formed a canopy of wet undergarments. Housed in an array of rusty, mismatched campers, the citizens of this traveling horde (circus junkies, proud itinerants, and illegal immigrants) could only be called by one name: Gypsies. Hugo and Victor, the only jesters in the Bosco Brothers Circus, were the first on this troupe to face the new day. Tripping on the only step to their cramped trailer, Victor managed to maintain control of their two tattered lawn chairs. Hugo, the more coordinated of the two, made a graceful exit, despite balancing a cardboard box full of grease paint, colorful marker paint sticks, and a used sock filled with baby powder. The twin brothers maneuvered their way across the rain-soaked gravel courtyard, and despite the dripping canopy of soaked underwear, they were able to find a dry spot near the center of the compound. The brothers placed the lawn chairs face to face and sat down to the business of painting each other's faces.

 Hugo and Victor could not remember the first time they painted a face with white grease paint, nor could they recall the first time they saw their father pull a trick out of a hat. Ten generations of jesters stretched across Hugo and Victor's family tree. Their branch on that tree was their heritage, and the mastery of that jester vocation was their inheritance.

Born into the village of Les andelys, Normandy, on July 4, 1885, the twins' roots reached deep into the town's history. The citizens of the town had always respected and honored the family's juggling dexterity and magical abilities. In return, the twins and their ancestors had tried to make the children of the town smile.

By the turn of the twentieth century, the twins had inherited the family business. Their reputation grew as they brought their act to other villages in Normandy, and by the time World War I descended upon Europe, they were celebrities throughout France. Hugo and Victor spent the war years entertaining wounded Allied soldiers, which earned them silver fleur de lis medallions from a grateful French government. The twins spent the post-war years, the 1920s and 30s, entertaining not only all of France, but the entirety of Europe. By 1940, they were not only famous—they were rich, too.

July 4, 1940, seemed to be just another routine day in the lives of Hugo and Victor, but as they would discover, this day would not be routine. As usual, the twins staggered out from their sixteenth-century chateau at noon, maneuvered their way across the gravel courtyard, and sat down on their ornate iron lawn chairs under the canopy of a full-growth grape arbor. After toasting each other with glasses of the finest Bordeaux wine, the twins were rudely interrupted by an armor-plated Mercedes-Benz crashing through the iron fence that surrounded the compound.

By the late 1930s, fashionable bureaucrats were in short supply in Hitler's Third Reich. So, when the back door of the Mercedes creaked open and out stepped Rudolph, dressed in a double-breasted suit with matching black britches, a brown fedora, and a red swastika tie, the twins were certainly not surprised. Rudolph, a mid-level manager from the Propaganda and Entertainment Ministry, managed to churn his way across the gravel without scuffing his brand-new brown wing-tipped shoes or wrinkling his argyle socks.

Rudolph was the first to speak. "So, here we are, the famous Hugo and Victor at home. Pretty nice house for a couple of jesters, don't you think?"

Rudolph had come armed with a deal to offer the twins: they could keep their home and lifestyle if they agreed to perform at the Hitler Youth camps. The Nazi camps were seen as cold and militaristic, and the Propaganda and Entertainment Ministry wanted to portray a kinder and gentler image. After signing a three-year contract, the twins and Rudolph sealed the deal with a toast and a glass of wine.

Time, distance, and war can morph a life or two. By July 4, 1955, the twins were 70- year-old illegal immigrants rolling with a one-ring traveling circus across America's heartland. Their family roots had not transplanted to this new land, and their honored magical acumen was now a distant delusion.

Before Hugo rubbed, stretched, and pulled Victor's skin firm enough to fill in the crevasses and cracks of his brother's wrinkled face, he whispered, "Close your eyes." After smothering Victor's eyelids, chin, cheeks, and nose, Hugo managed to swab his brother's forehead with white grease paint, without touching the furrowed scars laid bare on his brother's bald pate.

Bouncing out of a brand-new Jetstream camper, parked just outside the encampment circle, the ringmaster, the owner of Bosco Brothers Circus (there were not any brothers, or a Bosco involved—the name just sounded clever), set his gaze upon the twins. Always in uniform, the ringmaster was dressed in glittery red coattails, dark blue britches, black high-heeled boots, and an oversized red rhinestone top hat. All of this on a 5-foot-2-inch frame. Using a three-foot-long riding whip for ballast, the ringmaster swayed across the courtyard to the twins' outpost.

"You boys are up pretty early, ain't ya?"

Neither Hugo nor Victor looked up at the ringmaster.

"I said—you up?"

Having finished painting the white grease on his brother's face, Hugo reached into his cardboard box and pulled out a rag to wipe his fingers clean.

"You boys been with us, what, three weeks now?"

Hugo dug into his box and pulled out a black grease pencil.

"You know, to be honest, us Americans just don't get all those jester tricks of yours."

With the black stick pencil in hand, Hugo moved in towards his brother's right eyebrow.

"I mean to tell ya, the juggling of the rubber balls and the unicycling are OK, I guess."

Hugo drew a lightning bolt two inches above his brother's right eyebrow.

"But I mean to tell ya—all those trickster maneuvers and clever card tricks you boys do just ain't very American, I want to tell ya. "

Hugo moved over to his brother's left eye and began to paint a cockeyed sliver of a moon three inches above Victor's eyebrow.

"I mean to tell ya—a kid up in the 25th row can't see what you're up to!"

Finishing the moon, Hugo then painted a diamond shape on Victor's left cheek.

"No one is smiling! No one is laughing at your stupid tricks! There is nothing funny about magic! And that, my dear French tricksters, is why we are here—we are here to make the children smile!"

After painting a smallish square on his brother's right cheek, Hugo reached back into his box and pulled out a purple stick pencil.

"And look at Victor! No red paint on his face! No silly exaggerated smiley face, no red eyebrows and not even a bubble red nose, for God's sake!"

Using his purple stick, Hugo painted a small dot on the tip of Victor's nose.

"You boys need to be more like Bozo and Clarabell! You boys should get some of those big floppy shoes and a bicycle horn. And chase each other around in circles."

Hugo drew on his brother's lips, tracing a thin line to mirror Victor's smile.

"And you should laugh like Woody the Woodpecker and squirt each other with seltzer water! Now that would be funny!"

Knowing full well that the traveling circus was too far into the summer season to replace them, Hugo stretched back into his lawn chair and looked up at the ringmaster for the first time.

"Mister Ringmaster, Victor and I are capable of juggling eight to ten balls at a time. We can spin a dozen plates on sticks at the same time. And we can perform magic tricks that defy logic and reason. These skills have been passed down to us by several generations of master jesters. Victor and I have managed to master and maintain these honored and ancestral skills without once cackling like a woodpecker or chasing each other around with a squirt gun. And, Mister Ringmaster, we will not dishonor or disrespect our mentors who passed on this sacred knowledge by painting silly red smiley grins on our faces."

Hugo stood up and pointed his finger at the ringmaster. "Our father and his father before him passed down the promise of our heritage and wrapped it in the guise of our vocation as jesters. We will not desecrate that lineage by stooping to the level of merely trying to make the children smile. Mister Ringmaster, we are not clowns—we are jesters!"

After the ringmaster stomped back to his Jetstream, Hugo reached into his cardboard box and grabbed a used sock filled with talcum powder. Stirring up a small cloud of powder, Hugo patted his brother's face with the sock, sealing Victor's mask for the day.

"I promise, Victor," Hugo said, "I swear that I will not sell out again. Never again will we be collaborators."

Hugo was aware of their situation: they were 70-year-old illegal immigrants, with no money and a boss who would put up with only so much disobedience. And, since they were in a traveling circus with one-night stands across the small towns of America's Midwest, there surely was only one solution to their conundrum: robbing banks.

The emerald-green pastures were dotted with grazing cattle and an occasional waving human being. Just beyond the pastures, the horizon offered church steeples, gingerbread-trimmed homes, snow-capped mountains, and puffy white clouds framed in a bright blue sky. Hugo and Victor had become accustomed to this postcard scenery as they rolled along the back roads of the Third Reich. From the beginning of May to the end of August of 1941 1942, and 1943, the brothers had been enlisted to shuttle from one summer Hitler Youth camp to another. Their charge was simple enough: making the children smile. But, despite their best effort juggling, unicycling, spinning dishes on sticks, sleight-of-hand tricks, and magic card gags, the twins had not yet made a single child smile.

Still, Hugo and Victor had one more opportunity to make the children smile. But as the twins rolled their 1942 Mercedes-Benz touring car across the threshold of Camp Berchtesgaden, the last summer camp of their 1943 tour, the prospects of even a stray smile seemed remote. Greeting the twins, the camp commandant stood in front and just out of reach of his 300 Hitler Youths. Dressed in brown shirts, gray kerchiefs, black shorts, and red swastika armbands, the ten- and eleven-year-old boys' cold stares were etched into their stone faces. Organized into a tight formation, the boys formed a ramrod-stiff wall of true believers. Exchanging a glance and a nod, Hugo and Victor understood that Camp Berchtesgaden, in the valley just below Hitler's vacation retreat home, the Eagle's Nest, was

an exceptionally long way from Normandy, France.

Camp Berchtesgaden, much like all the other summer camps that the twins had visited, subjected the twins to a welcoming parade. Standing on a splinter-filled reviewing stand, the brothers were situated on either side of the camp commandant. Dressed in his uniform of a peaked gray cap, black high-heeled riding boots, a brown shirt, black britches, a red swastika armband, and a black-dyed, harmonica-shaped mustache, the commandant stood as erect as his pot belly allowed. The twins were decked out in their work clothes: pink and blue striped britches, purple bloused shirts, and golden Arabian slippers, all topped off with emerald, green cone-shaped hats rakishly tilted over their white grease-painted faces.

Surely, it must be written down somewhere that the snare drum martial march rhythms reverberate through the bones of all Germanic peoples. A case could have been made for that theory in front of the review stand at Camp Berchtesgaden. Pounding out a thunderous martial beat, a drum line of fifteen boys set the tone for the welcoming parade. Maintaining a proper goose step march while holding your arm out in a Nazi salute is not as easy as it might seem. But with the help of the drum line's rhythmic cadences, the boys managed to not only goose every step while holding on to their salutes but also wave a Nazi flag or two for good measure. Certainly, even the most grizzled storm troopers would be proud.

With the dust from the parade still hanging in the air, Hugo and Victor began setting up shop on the reviewing stand. Meanwhile, the boys rattled themselves into a semiformal gaggle in front of the stand.

Standing at center stage, the commandant introduced the twins to the youths. "Sons of Aryans beware of what will be presented to you today! These two French jesters will tempt you with clever magic. Do not succumb to their evil tricks, do not laugh or even smile, because as we Germans know, magic is not funny!"

Pointing at Hugo and Victor, the commandant yelled out: "So, without further talk, give these French tricksters a proper Deutschland welcome!"

Along with a snappy Nazi salute, the boys yelled out a hearty "Sieg Heil! Sieg Heil!

Juggling live German hand grenades is never easy but doing it while zigzagging across a warped stage on unicycles was especially difficult. Hitler's youths showed their approval with a loud "Sieg Heil" and a snappy salute. Spinning porcelain plates on top of ten-foot poles was a hit as well. Again, the youths yelled out and saluted the twins' effort. And so, it went—all the gags and tricks the twins had up their sleeves were saluted and Sieg Heiled without a single smile to be had. Reduced to one final card trick, Victor scanned the youths for a participant. Standing on a table behind the cadets, a small child, dressed not in a uniform but in lederhosen, was stretching himself out to see the show. Victor waved to the boy to come up onstage. It turned out that the boy was the camp commandant's six-year-old son, Adolf. Once Adolf was on stage, Victor pulled out an old deck of playing cards. He asked the boy to pick one card from the deck. "Keep the card face down," Victor said. Victor turned his back to Adolf and the boy looked at the card.

"Alright, now show the cadets the card."

Adolf moved to the edge of the stage and showed the card (King of Hearts) to the youths. Moving back to Victor, Adolf handed him the card face down. Victor held the card up to his

grease-painted forehead and asked Adolf to raise his arms up and say Abracadabra.

"Abracadabra!" the boy yelled.

Victor put the card back in the deck and shuffled it once. Then he pulled out a card—the King of Hearts. "Is this your card?"

"Yes!" Adolf screamed.

Adolf's lips began to quiver and his teeth began to show, but just when he was going to smile, his father clamped his hand over his mouth and yelled, "Magic is not funny!"

The children of Camp Berchtesgaden shouted out, "Sieg Heil! Sieg Heil!"

Hitler's Youths lined the exit road, and when the twins rolled over the threshold of the camp, the cadets gave Hugo and Victor a final Nazi salute and a hearty "Sieg Heil!"

In less than two years, these same children of Berchtesgaden would be holding up their arms again, only this time these eleven- and twelve-year-olds would be crawling out from under the rubble of Berlin, surrendering to battle-hardened Russian soldiers. Dressed in too-large used uniforms and covered in dust, mud, and blood, these children of Hitler's Third Reich will be holding up their quivering and dirty hands in surrender. And with gunfire whistling over their heads and bombs exploding at their feet, these sons of Aryans will whimper, "Don't shoot."

The breeze scattered Hugo and Victor's hair in all directions, but the cool sun was not warm enough to transform their white painted faces. The driver shifted their vehicle, a 1942 Mercedes-Benz convertible limousine, into a lower gear as they torqued their way up a mountainside road. Since a cold stare could never be confused with talking, the twins' backseat escort did not say a word as they chugged ever closer to their destination. Dressed in a black double-breasted suit and a low-slung brown fedora, the escort's red swastika lapel pin was his only surrender to conventional wisdom. As the Mercedes shuttered to a stop just short of the tunnel entrance to Hitler's mountaintop home, the escort leaned toward Hugo. Sticking his pointer finger into Hugo's chest, he whispered into his ear, "Make the children smile."

Snuggled in the Bavarian Alps, Hitler's vacation lair was surrounded by ever-unchanging snow-capped mountains. Gurgling just below the lair, a meandering creek snaked through an unkempt pine forest. The critters that inhabited the forest, large and small, scurried with the instinctual routines of foraging, hunting, and grazing. And up on the lair's cobblestone veranda, Hugo and Victor scurried with their well-learned routines of setting up tricks, gags, and magic. Just this side of a formal ritual, the jesters and the wildlife had one thing in common: survival.

The managers and department heads of the Ministry of Propaganda and Entertainment grazed across the veranda of Hitler's lair. Dressed in their bland ties, black double-breasted suits, brown fedoras, and red swastika tie pins, the bureaucrats were gathered for their annual vacation retreat. Sipping their fruit punch and eating cream Viennese pastries, the bureaucrats paid no attention to the jesters' dish spinning, juggling, and card tricks.

Not all hands are alike. Hands can be long or short or hard or soft. Folded hands can pray, and fist hands can fight. And an extended hand can be friendly but also feared. Joseph

Goebbels, the head minister of the Propaganda and Entertainment Ministry, rummaged his way through the throngs of his bureaucratic toads with his hand extended out to greet. Bony thin and bulging with fat veins, Goebbels's hands were soft from lack of use, if not damp to the touch. Once the jesters were finally finished with their show, Goebbels approached the twins with his five-year-old son at his side. Extending his hand out to Hugo, he added a quick nod to his limp handshake. "Herr Jesters, thank you for your dedicated effort of entertaining the youths of the Third Reich. Helmut here has a medal, an Iron Cross, for each of you.

Little Helmut handed Hugo and Victor their medals. "Danke Schoen," he whispered.

Just as Goebbels and Helmut turned to head back to the punch bowl, Hugo said, "Wait, I've got a little magic for Helmut."

Hugo pulled out a deck of cards, and just like Victor had done with Adolph at the Berchtesgaden Summer Camp, he had Helmut pick a card. Hugo held it up to his forehead, put it back in the deck, and then shuffled the deck again. And just as Hugo began to pull out the correct card, Goebbels grabbed Hugo's hand, squeezing it in a vice grip, which caused Hugo to spill the cards across the veranda.

"Helmut, the jester here is trying to fool you. Do not fall for his tricks. He smeared face paint on that card of yours—it is a mere cheap trick and certainly not magic. There is no such thing as magic in the world—there are only the tricked and the tricksters."

As Goebbels turned his son away from Hugo and guided him toward the cream-filled pastries, he stroked his hand across his son's shoulder. It was with that same soft, bony, damp hand eighteen months later that Joseph would force-feed his six children arsenic, including his only son, Helmut.

After their show was finished, Hugo and Victor set off on their epic fall from grace. Sitting in the backseat of a 1942 Mercedes convertible limousine, the twins began a plunge down Hitler's mountaintop to the terra firma below. Much like an out-of-control windmill, the twins spiraled down the cut-back mountain road. Hugo spent his time holding on for dear life, while his brother picked at the red swastika embedded in the middle of his merit medal. Hugo leaned toward Victor. "That swastika is not going to go away."

Victor shook his head and then threw his Iron Cross over his shoulder and into the pine forest.

"We deserved better," he said.

The twins' final plunge to the bottom ended on July 4, 1944. Sitting on their iron lawn chairs in front of their sixteenth-century chateau, the twins sipped from glasses filled with Bordeaux wine. Decked out in white-face grease paint, the twins stretched their legs out, California style.

Time was now of the essence. "We sold out to those monsters, Hugo. Sold out! And for what? This house, the wine, these iron chairs? We are collaborators, we are traitors—we did not even make the children smile!"

"Always remember this, Victor, that no matter our circumstance and no matter our audience, we were bred to be jesters. We have no choice, Victor, we will always be jesters no matter where we are or in what time we dwell."

And then their time was up.

An American Sherman tank smashed down their iron gates, and the good citizens of Les andelys came charging into the twins' compound. Standing up to surrender, the twins were then dragged to the town's square where they were lined up with the town's other collaborators. Using rusty razor blades, the good citizens shaved Hugo and Victor's heads until a stream of blood ran down their white greased faces.

The French court did its duty by sentencing the twins to five years in prison. When Hugo and Victor were freed, they fled to America—to become illegal vagabonds.

Time does not always heal.

The plastic partitions between the three bins of guns were scratched and dirty. Like Hugo, customers had rummaged through the guns, looking for just the right size pistol, causing the bins to look scruffy. The small guns in the first bin were fine, but the triggers were too small for Hugo's fingers. The larger guns in the second bin were the right size, but they just did not look threatening enough. The largest guns, in the third bin, were too large for Hugo's jacket pocket, but the size would surely intimidate anyone enough to make a point. This Muncie Indiana, Woolworth's had all the tools Hugo needed for a proper bank robbery. He found a baseball cap to cover his scarred bald head and a pair of rhinestone cat-style women's sunglasses to camouflage his eyes. And now he had found a high-powered German Luger style squirt gun.

Almost from the very moment that the twins had staggered onto American soil, Hugo had come to appreciate the fine sugary taste of chocolate chip cookies. Some people (Victor) had even suggested that he was addicted to brown beauties. As luck would have it, Hugo's affinity for the golden cookies would be challenged right there at the checkout counter of Woolworth's. A glass jar filled to the brim with sugary morsels was strategically placed right next to the cash register.

So it was that Hugo exited Woolworth's with all the tools he needed for a bank robbery. He had a Chicago Cubs baseball cap, a dark-toned pair of sunglasses, a high-powered squirt gun, and a laminated white bakery bag filled with chocolate chip cookies.

Hugo had never robbed a bank, but he figured it was a simple enough thing to do:

1. Arrive ten minutes after the bank opens.
2. Wait for the security guard to go to the back room to get his first cup of coffee and doughnut.
3. Put on his baseball cap and rhinestone sunglasses.
4. Do not say a word to anyone.
 5. Place a folded laminated white bakery bag on the counter.

Then, hand the bank teller a letter of intent:

Good morning,

      PLEASE DO NOT BE ALARMED, BUT THIS IS A STICKUP.

      I HAVE A GUN IN MY JACKET POCKET, AND I AM POINTING IT AT YOU.

      PLEASE PUT ALL YOUR LOOSE CASH IN THE LAMINATED WHITE BAKERY BAG.

      HAVE A NICE DAY.

      Thanks,

      Mr. Bank Robber

It was common knowledge that Hugo never carried loose change. So, it was not too surprising that he had accumulated ten parking tickets, in ten different towns, while he was robbing ten different banks. As luck would have it, Hugo defied his instincts and remembered bringing a nickel with him when he robbed his eleventh bank. But Hugo's luck ran out when he walked out the front door of the bank and ran into the ringmaster, who was hawking tickets for that night's show. Pointing to Hugo's bulging laminated white bakery bag, the ringmaster asked, "What you got there?"

Just before Hugo high-stepped his way down the street and around the corner to his ticketless car, he held up his laminated white bakery bag and said, "chocolate chip cookies."

It was not even five minutes later that the security guard came bouncing out the front door of the bank and asked the ringmaster for help. "Say, Mister, have you seen anybody with a laminated white bakery bag come out of the bank?"

Pointing in the opposite direction that Hugo had run, the ringmaster said, "He went that way."

The lilac-less smell of lilacs permeated the ringmaster's Jetstream camper, and the Kresge framed art on the walls of the trailer contributed to its claustrophobic atmosphere, but Hugo's presence there was not to criticize the ringmaster's home. He was there for a reckoning.

"It looked like you had a lot of cookies in that laminated white bakery bag of yours, Hugo. The police have been sniffing around lately, Hugo. Seems there have been bank robberies in all the towns that we have visited."

"Victor knows nothing about the bank robberies—nothing, I swear."

"It seems to me that you don't have very many options, Hugo. You can surrender to the police or run from the law, but then you will be leaving your brother all alone in this world. Do you think Victor can survive without you, Hugo? On the other hand, you can obey my wishes, and all your misdeeds will be a secret between you and me."

"Or I can run away with Victor."

"Do you really think that Victor could live a guilt-free life, knowing that you two were running from the law? Seems to me you don't have a lot of options, do you, Hugo?"

The August heat had rendered the grease paint too thin to cover all of Victor's wrinkles.

"Too hot to paint, Hugo?" Victor asked.

Stretching and pulling at the crevasses and cracks on his brother's face, Hugo knew that it really did not matter.
"It will be OK, Victor."

Bypassing his brother's eyes and mouth, Hugo moved on to his black stick pencil. As he filled in the dark sections of his brother's face, he decided it was time for some truth. "Seventy years, Victor. We have never been apart—not in that camper, not on stage, not even in jail. Christ, the only time we are alone is in the privy. Maybe, it's time for a change."

Victor stretched back into his lawn chair and looked up at his brother. "Hugo, how many times have you told me that we were bred to be jesters? That is all we know."

Hugo grabbed his grease paint and stick pencil and tossed them into his cardboard box. Tucking the box under his arm, Hugo turned his back on Victor and headed toward the circus

encampment's exit, but not before he told his brother, "Victor, this moment may seem to be forever, but our future knows better."

And for the first time in their lives, Hugo walked away without sealing his brother's mask with talcum powder.

Victor stood alone in the middle of the one-ring circus. The single spotlight shone down on him as he unicycled around the mounds of pony dung that had just been laid down by Bob's Dog and Pony Act. The silence of the audience was so loud that a child up in the 25th row of the bleachers could be heard yawning. The ringmaster stood in front of the crowd with his megaphone held up to his mouth. "Ladies and gents, Bosco Brothers Circus proudly presents Lackey the clown!"

With that announcement, the spotlight panned over to the door of the gym, and out bounced Lackey the clown, who had flamed red hair, a giant red nose, and a big red smiley face. With a bicycle horn blasting and his squirt gun blazing, his entrance took the crowd by surprise. The audience roared as he began to chase Victor around the ring, and everyone jumped for joy when Victor slipped on a pile of pony dung and fell into a fetal position on the ground. Lackey stood over Victor and squirted him on the face until the greased paint began to melt and drip down his baggy jowls. Victor looked up at his tormentor and asked- "Hugo is that you?" The ringmaster twirled his three-foot-long whip over his head, and Lackey waved his German Luger style high-powered squirt gun over his head and cackled just like Woody the Woodpecker. The crowd howled their approval, and the children, even the children up in the 25th row, smiled.

Half Moon

Antiquity knew this place. Prairie grasses swirl and bend to the feckless rhythms of the wind. The shadows, mirrored by unpredictable cloud formations, dart this way and that across the flat landscape. Purple, yellow, and blue flowers demand attention among the domesticated, drab prairie grasses. The land-based critters of this treeless land obey their inherited instincts by scurrying behind the swellings and contractions of the bellowing grasses. Speckled across the horizon, farmhouses and their barns sprout up like puffballs. Looking like prehistoric birds feeding on prey, not-so-occasional oil jacks move up and down, sucking the life out of this ancient terrain. Time has not stood still, but no one has bothered to tell antiquity.

Like roadkill, the Wayfarer was laid to waste on the shoulder of a remote county road in the middle of a Texas prairie. But unlike a squished armadillo, his tricolored van was still on life support. Unlike Magellan, the Wayfarer did not have a compass or a sextant to help him negotiate his way across an unknown landscape. His only navigational tool was his overused intuition. Not only was he adrift in the middle of a Texas prairie, but he was also hopelessly lost. One after another, measured by the fingers on one hand, fellow sojourners drove past the Wayfarer without a glance. Maybe the HELP sign he was holding was misspelled, or his long hair and scraggly beard drew negative attention, or the bright-red roses painted on the sides of his van did not fit a patriotic color scheme. But, then again, his invisibility was expected.

There are advantages to being stranded in the middle of a prairie. For one, you can spot a line of thunderclouds brewing on the distant horizon. The blood-red clouds rattling toward the Wayfarer were a curiosity for sure, and their color certainly added a biblical dread to the Wayfarer's predicament. The lightning jumping from one red cloud to another gave the good book's fire and brimstone an unwelcome validity.

But then, just on this side of the storm, an apparition of sorts appeared on the horizon. As with any ghost rider approaching any protagonist, the clarity of the Wayfarer's circumstances became more unambiguous by the minute. Once the lavender-colored station wagon pulled up behind the Wayfarer, the fact that it had no flashing lights or sirens provided some relief, and the hand-painted half-moons on the vehicle's doors and hood gave it a bona-fide ambiance. Of course, the four-foot-long loudspeaker on the crown of the roof reminded the Wayfarer of a Freeze Cream ice cream truck.

"You look like a weirdo!" yelled a voice over the loudspeaker. A pregnant moment of silence followed, and then: "Well! Are you such?"

 With the red storm gathering steam, the Wayfarer shrugged his shoulders and said, "Maybe."

The Constable, the voice behind the loudspeaker, yelled, "Get in the backseat before you and that hippie van of yours are blown adrift by the storm." The Constable must have had a premonition, because the red storm hit just as the Wayfarer crawled into the backseat of the half-mooned station wagon. Like a swashbuckling pirate captain, the constable gripped the steering wheel of his vehicle with the authority and acumen of a seasoned buccaneer. This image suffered a bit, however, because his posture and face resembled an overripe toad. But as the storm rocked his vehicle to and fro, the Constable added to the salty pirate impression by yelling, "Well shit!"

The storm's brutal visit lasted no more than a nightmare, but the damage was evident. Not only had the Wayfarer's hippie van been tossed into the roadside ditch, but his HELP sign had blown away into the grasslands. Contributing to a possible legendary fable or two, the half-mooned station wagon was no worse for wear. Wiping away the last few drops of rain on his windshield with a single swipe of his wipers, the Constable pulled out onto the highway and headed home to Half Moon, Texas.

"I'll send out the Fixer to get your hippie van," the Constable said. "You can stay at the shunning house until the van is fixed."

The Wayfarer shrugged his shoulders and said, "Alrighty."

There were not any gates, walls, or moats at the entrance to Half Moon. A watch tower might have been more dramatic, but the large gymnasium bordering the town was formidable. The signage on the front of the lavender-colored building named its function: Tidily Hall. The sign on the front lawn was informational: Fish fry and shunning tonight at 6:30. Bring your own forks.

The squared-off pattern of the streets of Half Moon gave it the symmetry of a chessboard, but the darkness created by the canopy of maple, oak, and birch trees that lined the streets added mystery to the scene. The homes in town were identical—1890s Victorian houses with wraparound front porches, all painted lavender with white trim. Matching Kentucky bluegrass lawns and freshly painted white picket fences surrounded each homestead.

Since red storms blew through Half Moon about as often as a blue moon graced its skies, the Constable decided to tour the town before he deposited the Wayfarer at the shunning house. Just this side of ritual, but well within his daily routine, the Constable eased himself into the drive-about. With his left hand wrapped around the steering wheel and his right hand cradling the loudspeaker's mic, the Constable twitched his head back and forth as he rolled slowly down the streets.

I suppose it would have been easier to identify each home in Half Moon with a unique lawn ornament or a numbered address, but the Grand Winker had decreed that each dwelling was to be named according to the temperament of the house's occupants. So it was that the cheesy placards enshrined on the front gates of each home proclaimed the organic psyche of the homesteaders inside. As the Constable inched down the streets, the Malcontents, the Dullards, and the Ninnies were scurrying across their front lawns picking up fallen debris. Always helpful, the Constable yelled out encouragement: "Don't forget the twigs!"

It was not surprising that the Constable slammed to a stop in front of the Bellyachers' dwelling. Not two weeks before, he had cited them for not keeping their lawn trimmed, and now they were nowhere in sight with a front lawn covered in debris. "Where, oh where are the Bellyachers?" he yelled. Showing a remarkable patience, the Constable waited twenty seconds before screaming into his loudspeaker again, "You two are in the deep!" Just as the Constable picked up his evaluation sheet, the Bellyachers padded out their front door and started to pick up the larger branches, but not the twigs, from their still untrimmed lawn. "I see how you are!" the Constable yelled as he wrote his judgment in big letters across his sheet: THE BELLYACHERS! --NOT WORTHY!

To say that time flies while driving through the streets of Half Moon looking for the Not Worthy is an overstatement. But then again, the village had just experienced a good-sized storm, and the Constable had a time-consuming knack for recognizing sloth when he found it. So It was that by the time the Constable had rolled past the last dwelling in town, occupied by the Nitwits, he had lost all track of time. Laying pedal to the metal, the Constable managed to screech up to the Tiddly Hall entrance just three minutes before the fish fry was to begin. After being commanded to "Get out of the car and go into the hall," the Wayfarer shrugged his shoulders and replied, "Oakley-Dokley."

Certainly, Tidily Hall's scoreboard and the adjacent replay screen had seen better days. But the enthusiasm of the Half Moon fans made up for any mechanical shortcomings. As the Wayfarer crossed the threshold of the hall, there was a large squeal from a crowd of fans gathered around a cloth-covered table situated in the middle of the hall.

 Sitting in a glass booth up above the hall, the play-by-play guy called out the winker's shot, "Oh my God! Can you believe it! I am speechless! I don't know if I have ever seen a shot like that!"

Red-faced and panting, the play-by-play guy tried to calm down. "OK, OK, let us just look at that shot in slow mo." The fans, numbering in the dozens, turned and looked up at the aging replay screen.

"Looky here, ladies and gents, a rookie, for God's sake, flipped that wink with the authority of a Winker Meister!"

As the slow-motion camera followed the flight of the white wink flipping its way to the lavender pot in the middle of the table, the crowd held its breath. And when the wink hit the back of the pot and rattled in, the crowd roared with delight. This was Half Moon tiddlywinks at its best.

The Tiddly Hall scoreboard, which hung down from the rafters, had kept track of hundreds of tiddlywinks contests, even the tri-county championships. But its main function on this night was to keep time for the fish fry. Once the horn sounded, the Half Mooners had exactly thirty minutes to get their fair share of fish, eat all they took, and dispose of their paper plates.

Conveniently, the scoreboard kept track of the seconds as well as the minutes left until the horn sounded that time was up. By the time the Constable had settled the Wayfarer into the darkest corner of the hall, the clock had ticked down to twenty minutes. And when a Lavender Bonnet (yes, she wore a lavender bonnet) finally showed up with a plate of fish parts, the clock was down to fifteen minutes. "Don't dawdle!" she said. With her arms folded in front of her, the Bonnet stood over the Wayfarer as he choked down the fish parts. "Faster! Faster!" she encouraged as the clock continued to roll. With one minute left on the clock, the Bonnet got down on one knee and leaned into the Wayfarer's face. "No slurping! Eat all the parts!" she yelled. Sounding much like a countdown to a moon launch, the Bonnet counted off the last seconds of the fish fry: "5-4-3-2-1." The scoreboard horn blasted. With fish parts hanging from his mouth, the Wayfarer was gasping for air as the Bonnet snapped his greasy plate from him. "Weirdo!' she said.

Moments after the scoreboard horn sounded, the play-by-play guy extinguished the hall's lights. Then, all together, the Half Mooners sat down in place. Once a respectful silence was achieved, the house spotlight was flicked on and beamed down on the Grand Winker, who was standing at the rear of the hall's stage. He was dressed in a white suit trimmed with gold tiddlywinks medals across the chest, with a lavender beret on his head. In unison, the citizens of Half Moon stood up. Battling his serpentine gait, the Grand Winker levitated his arms to keep his balance as he stumbled toward the stage. Upon his arrival at the podium, the Grand Winker lowered his arms. As one, the congregation sat down.

Certainly, a class or two in public speaking might have provided the Grand Winker with charisma.   But his folksy style of speech gave his minions a comfort level that allowed them to sit back and believe every word he uttered. "Good citizens of Half Moon," the Grand Winker began calmly, "we have a virus among us tonight"

The hall's second spotlight was turned on and beamed down upon the Wayfarer, who was sitting at back of the hall. "Just look at him!" the Grand Winker yelled. With that invitation, the entire congregation turned and stared at the wayfarer.

"Just look at him! Long hair, a scraggly beard! He is even wearing sandals! A daggum weirdo If there ever was one! Citizens, tell this stranger what you think of him!"

Altogether, the citizens of Half Moon stood up and yelled out in a rhythmic chant, "Weirdo! Weirdo! Weirdo!"

"Constable! Remove that stinking varmint from our presence!" the Grand Winker commanded.

The spotlight stayed on the Wayfarer as he was led out of Tiddly Hall by the Constable. With his head held high and his gait steady, the Wayfarer did not waver, even under the barrage of cries of "Weirdo! Weirdo!" as he was led out of the hall and into the Constable's station wagon.

"That weirdo won't be darkening our doorway anytime soon!" yelled the Grand Winker.

Half Moon, Texas, was incorporated on October 20, 1921. On the next day, the first Winker Meister of Half Moon won the inaugural tri-county tiddlywinks championship for the town. Despite droughts, floods, wars, and a depression, Half Moon continued to win the tri-county tournament year in and year out for the next one hundred years.

"Yesterday, October 21, 2021, will go down as the darkest day in Half Moon's history," the Grand Winker said. "For one hundred years we have never lost the tri-county tiddlywinks tournament until yesterday." Pointing to the darkest spot on the stage, the Grand Winker continued, "There is only one person responsible for that loss, and he is standing in judgment before me!"

Standing in the darkness and just to the right of the Grand Winker was the twelfth Winker Meister. From the time he was a boy, the Twelfth had never wanted anything other than to be a Winker Meister. Chosen by the elders of Half Moon to be the next Winker Meister of the town, the Twelfth had dedicated his life to the difficult discipline of tiddlywinks. He was taken from his parents at two years of age and trained daily in the finer nuances of the art of winks. Now, at the age of forty, he had no family or friends, and all he knew or cared about was tiddlywinks. In his twenty years as the Winker Meister, the Twelfth had never lost a tiddlywinks match, let alone a tournament.

A spotlight's glow can enhance one's appearance or reveal its drabness. Although the Twelfth's gold beret glowed in the light of the moment, his official lavender tracksuit looked shabby. When the spotlight shone down upon him, his knees buckled in the glare.

"Citizens, the Twelfth claims he lost the tournament because he sneezed and his squidge slipped from his finger, causing him to miss the winning wink shot." The Grand Winker stopped to shake his head.

"Did he lose to Full Moon? Nope! Did he lose to Quarter Moon? Nopper! No, sir, our Twelfth lost to the lowest of the low—Crescent Moon!" Stopping to catch his breath, the Grand Winker looked out at his congregation before continuing. "He sneezed for crip sake! Citizens, the Twelfth is not worthy of his title. He will have to pay a price for his imperfection. I hereby sentence the Twelfth to six months of shunning. Constable! Defrock our twelfth Winker Meister!"

A drumroll would have been the proper complement to the occasion, but a gasp from the audience dramatized the moment sufficiently. Appearing from the darkest part of the stage, the Constable carefully removed the Twelfth's golden beret. "Constable, shackle the Twelfth's ankles!" The Constable's lack of agility was apparent as he belched out a grunt as he knelt to clasp the leg irons on the Twelfth's ankles. "Constable, lead this unworthy one to the shunning house!" The congregation stood up and turned their backs on the Twelfth as he was led out of Tidily Hall and into the Constable's waiting station wagon.

Certainly, Half Moon's shunning house was in the top percentile of shunning houses. Sure, the front yard was covered with weeds and crabgrass, and the 1955 ranch house could have used a fresh layer of olive-drab paint, but the Porta-Potty on the front porch was clean as a whistle. And the ten-foot-high chain link fence that encircled the house was only five years old.

 The shunning house was only a two-minute drive from Tiddly Hall, and the Constable did not talk or even look at the Twelfth and the Wayfarer until he pulled into the circular drive that fronted the house. After ushering his two unworthy prisoners into the house, the Constable, even though he had never trained to be a docent, proceeded to point out the various features of the house. "There is no kitchen, bathroom, bedroom, or meditation room. And there aren't any TVs, radios, books, computers, video games, or tiddlywinks sets. Enjoy your stay!" As he was about to leave for his nightly rounds of the city, the Constable pointed at the 1950s plastic-covered living room furniture. "Be careful, that couch is lousy and full of rodents."

Vampire bat caves are not only dripping in blood, but they are also considered the darkest place on earth. Half Moon at night, with no streetlights, traffic lights, or porch lights, was a close second. As the Constable pulled away from the shunning house on his nightly drive-about, daylight had disappeared, and a carpet of fog smothered the streets. Half Moon, Texas, on this night was bat cave worthy. It was hard enough to herd the citizens of the town back to their dwellings after a Friday fish fry, but on this night the atmosphere in town was downright ghostly.

As the Constable turned on to Harmony Road, he noted a slight ripple in the fog. As he approached the apparent apparition, he began to slow down. When he pulled up to the ghost-like figure, the apparition turned toward his station wagon. The figure motioned for the Constable to lower his window. Sticking his head into the half-moon mobile, The Fixer, who was walking home, said, "Could use a lift home."

The Constable, relieved that the Fixer was not a ghost, said, "Sure enough." The town of Half Moon was small, so the ride to the Fixer's dwelling did not take long, and since the Constable's general mode of conversation was through his loudspeaker, the lack of small talk was to be expected.

"I just left that hippie van at the shunning house for that weirdo guy," said the Fixer.

 "Good," said the Constable. "The sooner that weirdo is out of town, the better."

The Fixer's dwelling was in the back of his business, and the Constable was able to drive right up to his back door. As the Fixer turned to get out of the Constable's station wagon, he leaned forward and added an afterthought, "I don't know if it matters, but there wasn't anything wrong with that hippie van. As a matter of fact, that van was not a hippie van at all."

 Surprised, the Constable asked, "What do mean?"

"Well, sir, that van has a super-charged engine in it. I'll bet that baby could go 150 on the open road."

Like a maximum-security prison, Half Moon's shunning house had all the bells and whistles: a ten-foot-high chain link fence with barbed wire sprinkled on top, an electrified gate, sirens, and searchlights. The only thing missing, due to a budget shortfall, was a machine gun tower. After dropping off the Fixer, the Constable hurried back to the shunning house as fast as the fog would allow. When he pulled up to the compound, he let out a whistle of admiration. Not only was the gate smashed open and the searchlights crisscrossing the compound, but the sirens were also screaming. And, like apparitions, the Wayfarer and the twelfth Winker Meister had disappeared into the fog of the night.

"Damn!" said the Constable. "We got to build that machine gun tower ASAP!"

Just a few miles outside of Half Moon, the fog had dissipated enough for the Wayfarer to crank his van up to that mythical 150 that the Fixer had fantasized about. Despite an occasional pothole and the super speed of the van, parts of the electrified gate stubbornly clung to the van's grille, giving off a mind-numbing rattle that would drive anyone to distraction. Anyone did not include the Wayfarer as he leaned over his steering wheel with an intense focus that could only be matched by the meditations of a devout monk straddling the edge of a cliff-dwelling cave.

As the van roared down this straight-as-an-arrow prairie highway, the Twelfth had many questions for the Wayfarer. For instance, where the heck where they headed? But after twenty years of competitive tiddlywinks tournaments, the Twelfth recognized the Wayfarer's intense focus. This was not a time for idle chatter. The Twelfth kept his trap shut. After an hour of meditation, even the most devout monk will break for a snack of herbal tea, a cinnamon scone and yak butter, but the Wayfarer maintained his meditative pose and silence even after two hours of driving.

Despite all his training and all his years as a disciplined meister of the fine game of tiddlywinks, the Twelfth could not take a second more of the silence. He figured he had a right to know where they were headed. "Where the heck are we going?" he finally yelled.

The Wayfarer did not lose his focus or his hunched-over pose—he just pointed straight ahead and said, "to the light." Sure enough, a sliver of light could be seen shimmering on the horizon. As they drew closer to their destiny, the Twelfth noticed that the shimmering light had morphed into a throbbing pulse and the skyline over the city of light was littered with rainless blood-red lighting flashes. When they finally passed over the threshold and into the city, the pulsating lights turned out to be neon lights advertising greasy fast food, gyp joints, and illegal gambling halls.

"What is this place, and who are you?" the Twelfth asked.

The Wayfarer ripped off his wig and fake beard and pointed to the lit-up city. "Welcome to Blood Moon, Texas, a city built by and for ne'er-do-wells, and I am the beloved Lord Mayor." Lining the streets to greet the mayor and the Twelfth, the citizens of Blood Moon waved their fists in a defiant greeting that could never be mistaken for a welcome.

Planted at the center of Blood Moon was a large open-air coliseum. In a wink to the past, the exterior walls of the twelve-story building were lined with statues of past tiddlywinks heroes. The entrance was dominated by a large flashing electric sign describing that evening's entertainment: Cheer our brave tiddlywinks gladiators as they shred that evil smarty-pants elitist Twelfth Winker Meister of Half Moon!

 Roaring through the main arched entrance to the arena, the Lord Mayor pulled his van up to a podium. Waving to the screaming spectators in the bleachers, the mayor grabbed a microphone and yelled out, "We got our man!"

Two thugs pulled the leg ironed Twelfth from the van. The spectators began to chant, "Shred the Twelfth! Shred the Twelfth!"

Waving his hand in the general direction of the dirt floor, the Lord Mayor yelled, "Let the games begin!" Just as he waved his hand, a large trap door opened in the floor, and twenty-five winkers dressed in blood-red tracksuits and black berets came marching up into the arena. Waving to the winkers, the Lord Mayor leaned over and said to the Twelfth, "This, Mister Twelfth, is your Armageddon!"

The Twelfth turned to the Lord Mayor and pleaded, "These leg irons are cutting my ankles. I'll never be able to concentrate in a tidily match."

The Lord Mayor smiled and replied, "Good, good!"

Antiquity knew this place. An oval coliseum dominated by arched supports. Flagpoles sprinkled across the top of the stadium, bending to accommodate blood-red pennants snapping in the Texas prairie wind. Filled with soul-bending resentment, the spectators in the bleachers had fire in their eyes, laughter in their throats, and contempt in their hearts. Gesturing with their hands toward the Twelfth, the spectators pointed their thumbs downward. Time has not stood still, but no one has bothered to tell antiquity.